Suddenly Marc's arms went around her

He drew her close, and his fingers went to her hair. His warm fingers on her scalp caused Meredith to bring her arms up and cling to him. His lips went down on hers, and she moaned very softly.

The silence of the forest engulfed them. Against her mouth Marc murmured, "I want you so much. Another five minutes of this and I won't hesitate to undress you, Meredith, and make love to you."

She felt the increasing excitement of desire. At last, she thought a little wildly, she was free. Free to love. For she had no doubts she had met the one man to whom she wanted to give herself. What happened afterward was of no importance.

Wayside Flower

Wynne May

Harlequin Books

TORONTO • NEW YORK • LOS ANGELES • LONDON
AMSTERDAM • PARIS • SYDNEY • HAMBURG
STOCKHOLM • ATHENS • TOKYO • MILAN

Original hardcover edition published in 1982
by Mills & Boon Limited

ISBN 0-373-02548-3

Harlequin Romance first edition May 1983

CHAPTER ONE

MEREDITH COTSWOLD cradled her glass of cool fruit juice in both hands and looked at the scene before her. Beyond the pool terrace of the Hotel Casuarina the curved white beach, with a grove of coconut palms fringing it, caught the shifting breezes that drifted across the lush and mountainous island of Mauritius. The air seemed intoxicating, love-spiced almost, and she breathed deeply.

Quite simply, and signed by 'The Management', the card had stated: Join us for cocktails at the pool terrace. And so here she was, wearing her black chiffon which had a drawstring neck and which was printed with great butterflies in shades of melon and deep emerald and falling in handkerchief points to almost ankle level. She was a stranger—amongst strange faces and she sipped her drink and gazed about her.

'So? You, too, have an appreciation for butterflies?'

The silver bangles on her wrist made fragile, jangling noises as she turned in surprise.

There was an aggressive air of confidence about the man who had spoken and she felt a sense of excitement at being singled out by one as good-looking and certain of himself.

Gathering her wits together, she gave him a brief smile.

'They seem to amuse you.'

'But no, on the contrary. Let us start with this. Here, in Mauritius, we have some very beautiful butterflies. I believe, in fact, that we have about thirty species.' His dark, tawny-flecked eyes travelled over her cocktail dress before coming to rest on her face.

'Really?' She could feel herself drowning in his gaze

as his eyes came up to meet her own. She took a "recovery sip" of her drink and the tiny, jangling noises
caused by her bangles had the power to remind her
that, except for her personal belongings such as clothes
and trinkets, she was very much alone here on the
island. 'Tell me about them,' she invited.

His eyes were mocking as he went on, 'Well, there is
a black butterfly. It has green dots and is known as the
swallowtail. It has a more complicated name. Let me
see if I can remember ... Papilo, yes that's it. And
then there is the Neptis ... how am I doing?'

'Very well.' Meredith smiled and bit her lip and
went on studying him with her beautiful green eyes.

She watched him as he slipped his fingers into his
glass and lifted a cube of ice from it, then he dropped
the ice back into the glass and his eyes came up to
meet hers.

Over and above the sound of conversation, punc-
tuated by laughter, which was going on around them,
the ice made a tiny explosion of sound.

'Why did you stop?' she asked.

'I have run out of butterflies.' He shrugged. 'I knew
this would have to come, of course.'

She found herself laughing.

After a moment he said, 'You, of course, are a visitor
here, no?' She was aware of his dark eyes going over
her and, although she had as much self-confidence as
most young women of her years, she felt uncomfortable
at his frank, appraising scrutiny.

Trying to sound careless, she said, 'Does it show
that much? But yes, I am a visitor.' There was a brief
silence. 'And you?'

'Me?' He lifted his shoulders and smiled, 'Oh, I am
a sugar planter on—what you say—a mini-vacation.
Only two days, in fact.'

Her whole mood changed. 'A sugar planter? A sugar
farmer, you mean?'

'Does that surprise you? But yes, I see that it does.

Why is this? I am curious.' His sudden, intense glance caused her heart to accelerate. As it so happened, it was the very last thing she expected to hear him say.

'It's just that you didn't strike me as being a sugar planter.' She made her voice light and casual, but she was inwardly tense.

'I inherited a sugar plantation from my grandfather,' he told her. 'The point is, I was willing to come from France to try such a thing. That was,' he lifted his shoulders and dropped them again, 'oh . . . four, five years ago.'

Meredith put out a feeler. 'In that case, you must know all—or most, at any rate, the sugar farmers in Mauritius?'

'Who, in particular, are you looking for?' He sounded amused, but his eyes searched her face.

'I didn't say I was looking for anyone in particular.' Nervously she lifted her glass to her lips and the fragile silver bangles on her wrist jangled again.

'Then why don't you look at me when you say this?' he asked.

Lifting her lashes, she said, 'I was merely curious. Making conversation, really.'

'So?' His gaze raked her. 'You know, your eyes are most disturbing. Do you know this? One glance across a crowded room should, I imagine, have had the power to intrigue many men.'

At that particular moment the manager of the hotel approached them. 'Ah, Merry,' he said, 'I was looking for you, but I see you have already started to mix. That is good. So, I leave you to enjoy yourself.' His smile embraced them. 'You must take her on a tour of your sugar plantation. How are your glasses? Do not allow them to remain empty.'

When he had gone Meredith drew a little breath and smiled at her companion uncertainly. 'Give me your glass,' he said. 'I will fetch us something from the bar. What were you drinking, by the way?'

'I was drinking a fruit juice.'

His fingers brushed her own as he took the glass from her and, to her surprise, she found herself shivering slightly and bit her lip. One hand went up to the nape of her neck, beneath her tawny-blonde hair.

From where she was standing, she watched him go in the direction of the bar. He moved, she noted, with superb grace, coming across as a kind of thrilling menace. He generated an atmosphere of excitement.

When he joined her again he was carrying two glasses in which ice tinkled as he walked. As he passed her a glass he said, 'You are a ... chic columnist, maybe?'

She laughed at that. 'This is most illuminating. What makes you think I may be a chic columnist?' Her nerves were suddenly on edge, however.

His dark eyes went over her briefly. 'A beautiful woman, set off by a sleek tan and who knows how to dress and wears earrings made of amethyst and crystal, is, to my way of thinking, a chic columnist.'

'Had you not considered the possibility that I might just be a very ordinary holidaymaker?' She spoke with a shade of annoyance.

Cradling his glass, he said, 'I had considered the possibility, yes, but somehow I do not think so. You appear far too *alert* to be a very ordinary holidaymaker.'

'Alert? That is a funny word to use. Actually, I do happen to be spending a short holiday—like you—at the hotel. The word island, I always think, carries with it a suggestion of romance, lesisure and adventure, maybe. I wanted very much to come.' This part, at least, was true, she thought. Richard Parker, her sugar magnate boss in South Africa, had suggested that she should spend a few days at the Hotel Casuarina before taking up her position as a chemical laboratory assistant on the sugar estate and where, incredible as it was, she was to act as a kind of spy for him. Suddenly the whole thing seemed highly dangerous and intolerable to her.

At first reluctant, she had, however, allowed Richard Parker to talk her round into applying for the job which had appeared in the Financial Mail section of a newspaper. The arrangement was that, on securing the position, she would work in Mauritius, using her position there as a stepping-stone to discovering the whereabouts and habits of Richard's grandchild. The child, a girl aged two years, had been born, out of wedlock, to Richard's only daughter Judy, and had been abducted by her father, André de Chavagneux, and taken from South Africa to Mauritius, which was his home. André de Chavagneux was the brother of the owner of the sugar estate in Mauritius, and all information gathered together, by Meredith, was to be fed back to Richard Parker, who would then set into motion a scheme whereby the small girl would be kidnapped and taken back to her mother, who was only eighteen. At this stage, Meredith would resign from her job and return to South Africa to work again for Richard Parker. It had all appeared to easy and so feasible . . . at the time.

'But I find this extremely puzzling,' the dark stranger was saying now.

'Why do you find it puzzling?' Meredith felt an instinctive thrill of fear. 'What's so puzzling about it?'

'That the word island, for you, carries with it a suggestion of romance, leisure and adventure, you said, and yet you are going to be here for only a short time. But—er—perhaps you are hoping to combine your short holiday here with something else?'

'What, for instance?' She took a sip of her drink and the ice rushed up to her mouth before she could stop it and rattled against her teeth.

'Adventure?' The tone of his voice was mocking.

'What kind of adventure? Really, you're being quite ridiculous,' she laughed lightly.

'Let us assume that it has something to do with a

sugar planter.' His voice, now, could not have been more casual.

This can't be happening, she thought. Does he know? Her nerves constricted.

'Oh, come now. Just because of a chance remark that you possibly know most of the sugar farmers here?'

'Oh, I don't know.' He laughed very softly. 'It is interesting to speculate, and I enjoy speculating about a beautiful woman.'

'Is that the way it is? Well,' she sipped her drink and looked about, taking stock of the guests, or pretending to, at the pool-terrace bar, 'you could be wrong, you know. But speculate, if it pleases you.' Her heart was beating uncomfortably and her breath felt uneven.

'Your name,' he went on, 'it is very unusual, no? Merry?'

She turned her green eyes on him. 'I have no idea what's behind all this—but yes, it's Merry. And since you're so interested, my parents wanted something very simple.'

'It was chosen, no doubt, to go with a very long and very complicated surname. That usually seems to be the case.'

Ignoring his remark, she said, as carelessly as she could, 'I adore your island cocktails, with sprigs of this and twists of that. It's all very exciting to me.'

'I am pleased you find it so. Perhaps you will extend your holiday now?'

'Perhaps.' She gave him an exasperated look, although she kept her voice light and mocking.

Cocktail party snacks, small, salty and spiced and planned to give excitement to the palate, were being passed around by young Indian waiters.

'You know, there is nothing to prevent me from finding out your name. You realise that, of course? Why, in that case, do you not tell me yourself?' As he spoke he watched her with lazy interest.

'I don't know why it's so important,' she said, trying to sound very amused, 'but, in any case, it's—Merry,' she used the hotel manager's version of her name, 'Merry Richmond.' She instantly regretted the remark, but comforted herself with the thought that her mother's maiden name had been Richmond.

'So?' He turned his eyes directly and fully on her and then his look became more speculative and penetrating. 'Merry Richmond.'

'That's right.' She tried to keep her gaze steady.

The pool-terrace was crowded now and the faces there presented a shade of colour and colour spectrum that ranged from bronze, near white to white and black and, in the crush, Meredith found herself standing very close to the man beside her. The sky was streaked with flaming gold and, except for a faint murmuring out there on the coral reef, it was a calm evening. On the other hand, conversation and laughter was very loud. Suddenly, whether by accident or design—it was difficult to tell—he lifted his glass to his lips and his arm brushed hers. She was thrilled by a vague and sensuous tremor, conscious of the warmth of him through the sleeve of his silk shirt. Had he been aware of the slight shudder that passed through her? she wondered. Or, was it all one-sided? All she knew was that the warmth intoxicated her, and this feeling was heightened by the faint murmuring of the waves breaking on the coral reef and the rustling of the coconut palms.

'It is, nevertheless, important for me to introduce myself,' he was saying. 'You see, names mean something to *me*. My name is Serge Jourdan.'

How was it she felt so let down? The name Serge came as a disappointment, somehow. Serge. She repeated the name in her own mind. Well, yes. It was so different—like *him*.

'You must feel satisfied now,' she said lightly, 'since names mean so much to you.' Beneath the remark, though, there was a suggestion of panic, for she was not used to lying.

Serge Jourdan went on looking at her, while he swirled the liquid round and round in the glass he was holding. His face appeared slightly hostile to her now.

'Oh, yes. I am a very involved-with-names type of person. Does that disturb you?'

After a moment she said, 'No, of course not. I mean, why should it? But nowadays, people just don't bother about names.'

'And you are one of those people, beyond any doubt.' There was a marked intensity in the way in which he watched her. 'Unfortunately, so far as I am concerned, society has reached the regrettable stage when it no longer cares about such matters.'

'Well, after all, it doesn't really matter, does it?' Somebody crushed past her, causing her to move closer to him.

'You know,' he went on regarding her, 'this—unconcern for such matters could get you into trouble, one day. But, in any case, I always wish to know the name of a beautiful woman, before asking her to dine with me.'

'I,' Meredith shrugged, 'I'll be dining at the hotel, anyway, being a guest here.'

'I want you to dine with me, at *my* table.' He spoke with the voice of one who is accustomed to giving orders.

They moved together in order to make way for a waiter bearing a tray of island cocktails and big black and green olives. Meredith's green eyes went to her companion's finely modelled mouth and, suddenly, he placed an arm about her shoulder and the sensation was nothing short of riveting. 'Careful,' he said, while she tried to arrange her confused thoughts. The fact that he was a sugar planter and might well know Marc de Chavagneux was disturbing, for she realised that the chances of meeting him again were very real. What reason would she have to offer for lying to him about her name?

'I have a perfectly wonderful view of the palms and coral reef from my own table,' she spoke carelessly, mockingly almost. 'It doesn't make much sense moving to another table.'

'At night the view is non-existent, or had you forgotten?' He did not take his arm away.

Once again, silver trays were being passed round to guests. The snacks looked exciting—nuts, slices of vegetables dipped in chick pea batter and fried crisp, tiny spiced meat balls, small boiled potatoes and a choice of chutneys. There were pieces of boned chicken, rubbed with masala and obviously grilled.

After they had helped themselves to something and Serge had exchanged their empty glasses for full ones he said, 'So—we dine together.'

'Do we?'

'Yes, we do.'

The pool-terrace cocktail party was going with a swing. People had not split up into racial groups and there was the right amount of noise. Nevertheless, one found oneself being nudged about and, with an air of mastery, he suddenly caught Meredith to him. 'Come,' he said. 'It is too crowded here now. We will take our drinks down to the beach.'

The white, powder-soft beach basked in an almost orange-pink light. Soon it would be dark. There was an element of drama about the setting.

'This is better than being imprisoned behind a wall of human bodies, surely?' he said. 'So—does my plan please you?'

Meredith took a sip of her drink and looked at him over the rim of the glass.

'What plan?' Her voice was purposely innocent.

'That we dine together?'

'Well, no, it doesn't, actually.' She felt suddenly apprehensive.

'You are being troublesome. Why are you afraid of me?'

'For one thing, you speak with the air of a man who is accustomed to success with women. I am not sure what to make of you.'

'And you find yourself—resenting this?'

'Yes, I do. Obviously you are used to this sort of thing. I, on the other hand, am not.'

'But I do not understand. Used to *what* sort of thing?'

'If you *must* know—striking up a casual acquaintance with a strange person.'

'You have very strict codes, in other words?' He sounded frankly amused.

She could feel the weight of the remark settle upon her and took a steadying breath.

'Yes,' she murmured. 'At least, I hope so.'

He laughed then, and she discovered that he had an infectious and boyish laugh. 'So? This I find very interesting. But I appreciate this, believe me.' After a moment he said, 'I am well known here. I will not kidnap you, if that is what is bothering you.'

Her heart lurched sickeningly. 'Of course not. Don't be ridiculous!'

'Well then, we dine together.'

She had never met a man with such magnetism. He was, she thought, a man who would cause instant excitement—anywhere—under any circumstances.

From where they were standing they could see that, in the half-light, the pool-terrace with its palms, colourful cushions and sun-umbrellas and bar area, was beginning to empty as guests went to prepare for dinner. As a backdrop, one of the island's strange shaped mountains rose majestically against the translucent sky. The first stars were beginning to show and, in a few moments, the mountain would appear merely as a brooding bulk.

Serge Jourdan reached for her glass and his fingers

brushed hers and she realised that this was a game—one with an undercurrent of accepted intimacy on the part of both.

'Come.' His voice was soft.

They went back up the shallow steps which led from the beach to the lawn leading in the direction of the terrace. Meredith watched him moodily as he placed their empty glasses on the counter.

Then he came towards her, walking easily. The movement of his hips was disturbing. He was dark and elegant and there was a marked intensity, even in this light, in the way in which he watched her. There was about him vitality and something else—impatience.

He did not touch her, however, as they walked in the direction of the hotel which was built in local style with many arches and all the large and luxurious rooms looking out over the sea. All were air-conditioned, with private facilities and balconies. There were indoor and outdoor restaurants and a magnificent pool with an island bar and sunken bar stools.

Meredith lifted her hands to her hair which was blown about by sea-breezes.

'I'd like to go to my room first, if you don't mind,' she said.

'Of course.' He was at his most formal. 'I'll be waiting for you in the foyer.'

By the time she got back he was already there.

'So?' His dark, tawny-flecked eyes went over her. 'You have piled it high, your hair. I like it.'

'Thank you. It's cooler this way. I hope I did not keep you waiting too long?'

'If you did, my appreciation is high, believe me.' He spoke easily.

Instead of eating in the dining-room he took her to one of the restaurants where the cuisine was French and, later, they danced to a mean beat played by a band called Pearls of the Indian Ocean. At midnight Serge said, 'And now we will visit the casino.'

'Just like that?'

'What do I take that to mean?' he asked.

'I might not want to go.' She felt herself tightening up.

'If you don't, we will change that.' His eyes were mocking.

'I'd be a crashing bore. I'm absolutely ignorant so far as casinos are concerned.'

'So? What does it matter? A beautiful woman, set off by an exciting tan and who knows how to dress, adds to the excitement of any casino, without having to do a single thing.'

To indicate that she took his compliments lightly, she laughed lightly. Within her, there was the strong temptation to forget about Richard Parker and the *real* reason as to why she was here in Mauritius and resume her life as if her reason for being here had no reality other than to enjoy herself and to drift into a love affair with Serge Jourdan . . . no matter how casual.

In the end, however, he had his own way. The casino, to her way of thinking, was a place of intrigue and romance, even, where adventurers came to try their luck in an atmosphere of clicking dice, shuffling of cards and a steady undercurrent overplaying everything else.

At his insistence, she tried her own luck and was almost immediately swept out of her depth.

'Oh,' she wailed, dismayed. 'I've lost, haven't I?'

He placed an arm about her. 'So what? Come, you are not the only one to have lost at this game . . . the game of gambling. Do you know what Dostoevsky said, after losing?'

Laughing, she said, 'No. How should I know that? I told you, I'm really rather ignorant.'

'He said, and I think these are his very words, "The roulette wheel has no memory and no conscience," and that is bad, no?'

'What's bad?'

'To have no conscience.'

Her heart kicked over and she bit her lip.

'Would you like to swim?' he asked, when they were in the garden.

After a confused moment she said, 'Okay.' She said the word on a little breath, for she knew that if she knew what was good for her she would refuse. 'I'll go and change.'

When he knocked on her door she stood for a moment with her teeth pressed on her lip. She had already changed and was wearing an apricot-pink silk shirt over a brief dark brown bikini. She opened the door and their eyes met and held. For an instant she found herself not only disturbed by the frank assessment of his strangely flecked eyes, but a little angry. Before she could stop him he moved past her into the room.

Over swimming trunks, he was wearing a short striped towelling bathrobe. The robe hung open and she caught a glimpse of his chest and the dark, glistening hairs growing there.

'It is a logical conclusion that I am going to kiss you,' he said, very softly, 'again—and again.'

Things were working too swiftly for her, but at the same time she felt excited by him and her eyes widened, before going to his lips. Her lashes came down as he slipped his arms about her and her apricot-pink silk shirt fell open as, against all common sense, her arms came up and around his neck.

When he kissed her she kissed back with a wildness that might have come from someone else. 'And to think we were strangers a couple of nights ago,' he muttered, against her mouth. 'You excite me—I would like to keep you here all night in my arms.'

Suddenly the spell, for her, was broken. 'I've had too much wine with my dinner,' she said, moving away from him. 'Shall we swim?'

Feeling devastated and humiliated, she allowed him to lead her to the pool and then she watched him as he shrugged out of the striped bathrobe and dived into the black, glittering water.

Before he had time to surface she slipped off her silk shirt and dived in, after him, and then she did a slow crawl to the other side of the pool. When he joined her he said, 'You are as much at home in the water as you are in my arms.' He pressed her against the side of the pool, pinioning her there with his arms.

Music which was still being piped to the pool area from somewhere within the hotel added to the excitement she was feeling.

'Listen to the words,' he said, 'do you know them? You are a butterfly child, so free and so wild. It is very popular here at the moment, this song. Is that why you wear butterflies on your dress; because you are so wild and so free?'

'I'm not wild. I think you're detestable for saying that!' Meredith tried to wriggle away from him.

'You are a mixed bag of tricks, maybe?' His voice was hard and she felt cheated.

'I would like to go in now. I'm really very tired.'

'What about a Brandy Alexander?' He was smiling now.

'*What* about a Brandy Alexander?' she snapped.

'It will make you sleep like a little brilliant lizard in the sun. It is really a very good nightcap. Do you know what is in it?'

'No.' She turned away from him, preparing to leave the water.

Coming after her, he said, 'It is a somewhat rich concoction, I suppose, but it is really very good. It is topped with cream and chocolate flakes. I will fetch them myself and then, I promise you, I will let you go.'

'I'm not sure whether to trust your promises.'

He laughed at that. 'But no, I promise you.'

While he was away Meredith lay back on a reclining poolside chair and gazed up at the stars . . . a girl of long and slender bones and who was suddenly very confused and unhappy.

When he spoke she sat up abruptly. 'You gave me a fright! Do you realise that we're the only ones left? Everybody has gone to bed.'

He passed her the glass and she tried not to touch his fingers as she took it from him. He sat on the paved area beside her and then, over his glass, toasted her silently.

'Something is bothering you,' he said, after a moment, and the tone of his voice was half-way between a statement and a question. 'No?'

'Nothing is bothering me.' She was ill at ease and irritated. 'Except that I'm getting a little tired of all this.'

She drew in a sharp breath as he bent his head and rubbed his lips lightly against her thigh. A sudden demanding flame of longing leapt into her veins.

'To touch you is a pleasure for all the senses,' he said. 'You stimulate my senses—and my imagination, Merry. I do not think I will ever get used to calling you Merry.'

She moved her legs to one side. 'You know,' her voice was choked, 'meeting you has been a dust-devil experience for me. I'm not sure I like it. In fact, I'm sure I don't.'

'A dust-devil? What is a dust-devil?'

'It's a—whirlwind. Things have got out of hand. I mean ... to have established something—physical— like we have tonight, after only a few hours ...' she broke off.

'Is something physical so terrible?' She realised that in the filtered light of the stars and poolside lanterns, he was holding her gaze deliberately.

She set the glass down beside her chair and gracefully slid off the reclining chair on to her feet.

'Goodnight,' she said, stooping to retrieve her silk

shirt, 'and thank you for everything.'

Before he could change her mind for her she turned and ran in the direction of the hotel.

Before going inside, she turned to look back and saw him walking in the direction of the beach. Although of average height, he gave the impression of great physical strength, and she shivered slightly.

CHAPTER TWO

A GAUZY heat-haze hung over the island when Meredith awoke the next morning. It had been a deep, revitalising sleep and she lay gazing out of the wide sweep of glass which opened out on to her balcony. She tried to unwind her mind, slowly at first, languidly, taking in the breathtaking beauty of the sea, the white coral beach and those exciting, swaying palms. And then she thought about Serge Jourdan and experienced a physical weakening and she knew that she was well on the way to falling head over heels in love with him. It was something which had happened at first sight, but that did not mean that he felt the same way about her. A worried little frown caused her green eyes to change expression as she remembered how, at the casino, he had caressed his dice almost lovingly, watching her as he did so, with a devilish glint in his dark, unusually tawny-flecked eyes. At the thought that she, too, might mean nothing to him—just another dice to gamble with, she sat up and tossed the sheets to one side.

After a shower, brisk rub down and applying a body-spray and the exciting feel of silk, upon silk, upon her skin, she looked forward to the long, thrilling day before her. It was the leisurely toilet of a girl on the brink of love. Would he be there waiting at the pool-side, expecting her to eat breakfast with him at a table for two with a view of the palm-fringed beach and coral reef?

Serge Jourdan was nowhere in sight, however, so she went into the dining-room where sliding glass had been slid back to accept the island breezes. Tall, long-leafed pink and yellow lilies were intermingled with a heady assortment of fruits on the long buffet table, where Meredith started to help herself. Then she took a plate of fruit and a glass of fruit juice to her table, where she was later served breakfast. All the time her green eyes searched the space for Serge Jourdan.

Later she went down to the beach and slipped out of the pale pink organdie caftan she had worn over her bikini to breakfast. The tide pounded the reef and the beach was like creamy oatmeal. The hotel behind shared this magnificent setting with only a few private chalets.

During the course of the morning she could visibly notice the change in her tan, and she felt rested and her spirits began to lift. Perhaps he had slept late? Perhaps, in the end, it would all work out for her and, when they met again, she would be able to joke about having misled him about her name.

Two hours later, and after spending more time in the pool, Serge had still not put in an appearance, however. She wandered about the hotel gardens, admiring the pink, red, yellow and white hibiscus and pink oleanders. Shawls of bougainvillaea, in shades of mauve, purple, wine-red, orange and white, waved about in the breeze. She was dazzled with so much colour. And then she began to feel she had been abandoned.

Before lunch she took a shower and put on a heavy red silk caftan, which she wore with a romantic air. Her tanned feet were encased in high-heeled gold sandals, and when she went to the open lounge where she intended ordering a cocktail for herself before lunch, several men eyed her with interest.

Once again her green eyes searched the lounge, which was open to the sea-breezes, for Serge Jourdan. Where could he be? She came to the unpleasant conclusion that she had been used, just in the same way as he had used the dice in the casino, while he was in the process of winding up his short vacation.

'Ah . . . Merry.' It was the hotel manager who, for some reason known only to himself, had decided to abbreviate her name. 'You look so attractive. It is a pity, no, that he had to leave—but then a cane fire can play much havoc if not supervised immediately.'

Feeling suddenly wildly excited and happy inside, she said, 'I—didn't know, of course. So it was a cane fire?'

'But yes. When word came through on the phone he left for his estate almost immediately. But cheer up. Maybe he will be back before you leave?'

'I don't think so. You see, *I* leave in the morning.'

'Oh,' he spread his hands and bunched his chin, 'too bad, too bad . . . but why don't you stay on for a while longer?'

'I can't. I'm about to start work.'

'Here in Mauritius?' He sounded curious.

'Yes.'

'Well,' he spread his hands again, 'Mauritius is small, Merry, only a speck in the ocean. The chances are that you will meet him again—and again.' He spoke on a note of good-natured mockery and she felt very young and silly.

'Perhaps,' she replied, watching him moodily as he left her.

What if she did meet Serge Jourdan again? Was it not better, perhaps, that they did not meet again? For, what excuse could she give for lying about her name? She could, she supposed, shrug the matter away. She could say, quite simply, that she had not taken the interlude at the hotel all that seriously and that for a short spell the island had wrapped its magic about her without any thought of the morrow.

The fact was, of course, that when he had spoken to her at the pool-terrace cocktail party, she had been virtually swept off her feet and caught completely unawares when he had mentioned that he was a sugar planter. The chances that he would know Marc de

Chavagneux were very real, and the fact that she was
here to spy on Marc de Chavagneux and his family
and report back to Richard Parker was suddenly
frightening and deplorable to her.

What had she been thinking of, to agree to becoming
nothing better than a cheat? Brooding on this, she knew
that she had acted on good intentions, believing that a
small girl of two should be with her mother. In fact,
she thought now, it had nothing to do with her and
she had become a busybody and a cheat. The idea was
nothing short of revolting.

These thoughts still nagged her as she ate her lunch.

Serge Jourdan had still not returned to the hotel by
the time she left for the sugar estate the following
morning.

A courtesy mini-bus took her right to the estate. The
rambling white double-storey house stood at the end
of an avenue of palms. Wide steps led to the downstairs
veranda which ran the full length of the house, and a
veranda of the same dimensions above it was striking
with white, ornately scrolled wrought-iron.

It was, Meredith realised at once, a magnificent old
house which surely must have stood up to many a cyclone and which must have been a place of lavish
entertaining in the past and, no doubt, still was. Large
windows and many French doors were equipped with
louvred shutters to cope with tropical gales and possible cyclones.

In his formal letter appointing her, Marc de
Chavagneux had stated that she was to report for duty
at his home, after which she would be taken to the
accommodation which was being provided for her on
another part of the estate.

There were Indian straw chairs and split-bamboo
tables with plate glass tops on the long veranda. The
elaborate front door was guarded by two blue-and-
white ceramic elephants and it was opened for her by
an elderly Creole woman who guided her from a

spacious hall into an attractive lounge which, even to
Meredith's inexperienced eyes, had an eighteenth-century French look about it. There was, however, a
country-house atmosphere and the walls, which
possibly could be described as the shade of a rosy-ripe
mango was the kind of shade which would be enhanced
by an island sunrise or sunset. Low floral upholstered
sofas and other, more formal chairs were offset by good
furniture and rich paintings.

'If you will wait here. Monsieur is expecting you.
Please, however, he wishes for you to sign this book.'

Meredith looked at the woman in frank puzzlement.
'He wishes me to sign—a book?'

'Yes. Your name, please.'

'Oh ...' she broke off, flustered. 'I see.' But she
didn't. 'It must be a—register? Is it?' She smiled uncertainly at the woman.

'He did not say, but yes, it must be. He will be with
you shortly.'

Meredith's eyes went to the book, which was on a
low table between the low sofas, then she sat down and
drew it towards her. A pen had been provided for her
use and the book was new. Monsieur Marc de
Chavagneux must be a very staid old gentleman, she
thought, who would have strict ideas on this and ideas
on that.

She signed her name, M. W. Cotswold.

Wearing beige, which looked superb with her green
eyes, glossy hair and super tan, she sat gazing about
the gracious room when she heard a movement and,
turning, caught her breath when Serge Jourdan
entered the large room. She felt a shock of pleasure.

'What a coincidence,' she said. 'I—I didn't know
you knew Monsieur de Chavagneux.' She was flustered
now, wondering how to explain her false name to him.

'*I* am Marc de Chavagneux.' His voice was cold. It
was the voice of a stranger.

'But——' She swallowed and then stood up. There

was a silky elegance about her and she saw his dark eyes go over her. 'You—didn't—say. You told me that your name was—was Serge. Serge Jourdan.' Her mind was flailing about.

'Forget the games,' he snapped. He went to the low table and, stooping, picked up the small, expensively bound book. Tensely Meredith watched him, hardly breathing.

'This is your signature?' His thick dark lashes lifted and he regarded her accusingly. 'Your *usual* signature?'

'Yes, of course.' She felt suddenly quite and desperately ill. She thought she was going to faint.

He exuded authority and confidence. 'And yet your signature on your letter of application bore a very different handwriting. It was the writing of a man, in fact.'

'It was my signature,' she said softly. On Richard Parker's recommendation she had signed *Meredith W.* (for Wendy) *Cotswold*. Also on his advice, she had used a thick ballpoint pen, thus giving the signature a masculine appearance. This was done for a purpose because, although the application for a laboratory assistant had not stated whether the vacancy was for a male or female, it would reflect away from the fact that the application came from a young girl. This summing up, by Richard Parker, had caused her to believe that Marc de Chavagneux was an elderly sugar planter.

'Why did you deceive me?' he was demanding now. 'Why did you lead me to believe that you were a young man?' His mouth tightened with contempt.

'But I said nothing about being a young man.' She felt ready to fall apart.

'This name—*Meredith*—happens to be a man's name, no?' He tossed the book on to the table and it fell on the carpet.

She looked stricken. 'It happens to be *my* name, believe it or not. My name is Meredith Wendy Cotswold.

I'm sorry about the Merry part—but the manager back at the hotel started calling me Merry and I'm afraid I just allowed it to pass. Please try to understand . . .'

'I do not understand and I do not pretend to understand.'

'Oh, what's the use of going on?' she shook her head. 'You've closed your mind to all reason.'

'So? I have closed my mind to all reason? And what about—Richmond? You told me that your name was Richmond, no? In other words, you lied to me.'

Meredith went cold inside herself.

'It wasn't altogether a lie. My mother's maiden name was Richmond . . . I just decided to—to use it.'

'Why?' He gave her the benefit of those furious dark eyes.

'Well, if it comes to that, you lied to me,' she lifted a distracted hand to her tawny-blonde hair and his eyes followed the movement. 'You told me your name was Serge Jourdan.'

'When I signed the register at the hotel,' he said, '*your* signature was two away from my own. In the column provided there was your address. Your *full name* and address. *Miss* Meredith Wendy Cotswold. That was enough for me, and so I sought you out. In fact, you were pointed out, at my request, by the manager himself. You are no better than a jet-set Jezebell, out for a good time. Into the bargain, you are an impostor.'

'But this is ridiculous! I'm *not* an impostor. I am who I am. And *into the bargain*,' she initated him, 'your advertisement said nothing about the vacancy having to be filled by a male laboratory assistant. Therefore I'm not an impostor. Right?' She was shaking now, and spoke with an angry helplessness.

'Let me tell you something,' he went on, 'all applications were scrutinised—on a number of factors. I would, I am very sure, have discarded applications coming from the female sex—unless I had absolutely no choice. In fact, several applications came from women and they were, in view of the fact that there were several *male* entries, put to one side. Your application was considered along with several other entries ... all male. I considered your application to have been written by a man, in view of that thick signature and the name Meredith. Yours was chosen because of certain qualifications lacking in the others.'

'And so,' anger shot along her nerves, 'leading me on, one way and another, *you* lied to *me*. After all, your name isn't Serge Jourdan, is it? Besides, what difference does it make whether the job goes to a man or a woman? I do just happen to be a qualified chemist.'

'It makes a lot of difference,' he snapped. 'I made my plans accordingly. You were to share a house on the estate with a man who, so far as women are concerned, is a dangerous customer. Now you will have to stay here.' There was an arrogance about him, an aristocratic air of authority, which made her feel absolutely inadequate.

'So you are keeping me on? In other words, I'm to fill the vacancy?' Her anxious eyes went over his face.

'Much against my better judgment, yes. I have no time for deceit, and you have deceived me.' He spoke with measured harshness.

And how much had he deceived her? she wondered. For obviously, while he had been stringing her along at the hotel, there had been a wife here in the background. Without turning, she was aware of the flowers, expensive lamps and superb arrangement of furniture.

'Let us start somewhere,' he went on. 'A room has been prepared for you here. You will have your own bathroom.'

She held a brief consultation with herself—her thumb pressed between her teeth. Then she said, 'The odds are that I'll just leave here ... walk out and take the next flight home.'

'Odds can be upset,' he replied. 'You have been

appointed to this position and you will keep the appointment.'

Meredith realised that she was relieved in a vague, but very noticeable way. The reason was far from simple, but it existed all the same. She was already so fascinated by him that she lost all sense of logic in the pleasure of having met him again. She was resolved, however, never to give herself away.

'I would advise you not to lie to me in the future, *Miss Cotswold*,' he told her, and her nerves immediately constricted. 'You will discover for yourself that when provoked, I have a volcanic temper.'

'I realise that you're now my employer, and not just Serge Jourdan,' she ventured to say, 'but . . .'

He cut her short. 'I am glad you get the idea.'

She expelled an impatient breath and continued, 'As I was saying, *Monsieur de Chavagneux*, it cuts both ways. *You* also lied to *me*, no?'

'The difference being that it was a lie for a lie. *I* am not in the habit of lying and, for this reason, I do not hesitate to tell you that there will be dangers for you to stay in this house, but perhaps the risk will not be as great as it would be in the case of sharing a house with Gérard Catroux. I believe that I shall be more in control in a case like this, but the dangers exist, nevertheless.'

'What dangers?'

'There is much about you,' his dark eyes travelled slowly, almost insolently, over her, 'to delight the eye, and I shall want to make love to you.'

'In that case, you're no better than this—Gérard Catroux, are you?'

'I differ from him in one respect. Certain women appeal to me, at the time. I get so far and then I begin to lose interest. He, on the other hand, becomes very intense. His jealousy—his attacks of jealousy—are well known on the island. Perhaps the danger will pass. You *should* be safe here, but,' he shrugged maddeningly and her eyes watched him, 'you can never tell.'

Giving him a spiteful look, she said, 'I'll see that you're not seriously inconvenienced. I'll keep out of your way, as much as possible. In fact, I would prefer that. You see, as a man, I find you quite detestable.'

There was a feeling of unreality about the entire situation and the predominant thought was: I can't believe this is really happening to me. She realised that she should leave—and yet she wanted to stay. He was like a dark creature of the jungle, she thought, and she was easy prey, completely mesmerised. She shivered slightly.

'Lunch will be served at one o'clock,' he was saying. 'Emerita will show you to your room. Your luggage has already been taken there. After lunch, we will drive to the laboratory in which you are to work. You will be shown round and introduced to people.'

'Very well.'

The room to which she was shown came as a delightful surprise to her. The four poster bed was delicately draped and the fragile dressmaker-detailed treatment included a shirred dome-shaped under-canopy. A cheerful floral print upholstered the bed and the walls, showing off to perfect advantage the white drapes on the fourposter.

There were roses, camellias and azaleas in vases beside the bed and next to both vases rock-crystal elephants, with green jasper eyes, stared back at her. She noticed that Art Nouveau stationery had been placed on a desk.

Going to the windows, she gazed down at the extensive well-planned gardens and, in the distance, the cane which sloped down to the ocean. Several Indian women, wearing brightly coloured saris and floppy straw hats were working in the garden. The wide, shuttered doors were open, the shutters fastened back, to the veranda where crotons in huge white urns had been placed at intervals along the full length of the space. Indian straw chairs invited one to relax there. From the veranda the sight of glinting sugar cane sweeping down to gilt crescents of beaches, in the distance, and that shaded sapphire sea was a thrilling sight.

Glancing quickly at her wrist-watch, she hurried back into the room and began freshening up for lunch. There were tall flagons of colognes and oils, linen face and hand-towels and huge, fluffy bath-towels in the bathroom. The soap was Lanvin-Arpège, and when she noticed the Monsieur she bit her lip. Did *he* expect to visit her? Perhaps his wife was away? In France, maybe. Her cheeks grew hot. What had he called her? A jet-set Jezebel.

After a hasty shower she changed into a simple white voile dress which she knew was a very effective background for her tan, and then she went downstairs. In the hall she stood, uncertain and tense, and then she heard him call out. 'Come through. I am sure you could do with an island cocktail before your lunch.'

'Thank you,' she murmured, entering the gracious lounge, 'but I didn't expect to drink an island cocktail with you.' Her green eyes scanned the room for another woman.

'I am alone,' he told her. 'I live in this house alone.'

'At the moment, you mean?' she stammered, confused.

'What do you mean—at the moment?' He sounded half impatient, half amused.

'I thought that, under the circumstances, you must be married,' she replied, as he came towards her with her cocktail. When she took it from him she was careful not to allow her fingers to come into contact with his.

'I am afraid I do not understand. What—circumstances?'

'It just seemed—possible,' her voice trailed away.

'But no. There is no wife in my life. Apart from the coming and going of servants, we are quite alone here.' He took a sip of his drink and then shrugged carelessly. 'This is something like producing a play, no? In this case, only two characters. I am not sure whether the two people concerned can be described as the right cast of characters, at that.'

'I would like you to know,' she ventured to say, 'that, to me, Serge Jourdan was somebody quite different.'

'He exists, nevertheless, and we must try to keep that in mind,' he answered, giving substance to the words with his very reasonable and cultured French-accented voice. 'By the way, Serge Jourdan had to leave the hotel upon receiving news of a cane fire on the estate.' He smiled faintly.

'But he knew, of course, that little Merry Richmond would be turning up here.' She could not keep the sarcasm from the tone of her voice.

Louis Seize chairs surrounded the opulently draped oval dining-table. The subdued floral folds of the tablecloth touched the Persian carpet on the floor. At one end of the room an imposing antique armoire added height. It was a room glowing with soft colour.

While the first course was being served Meredith said, 'This is a beautiful house, Monsieur de Chavagneux—inside and out.'

'I am glad you like it.' He spoke with ease. 'I inherited a good many things, from my grandfather.'

When lunch was over he said, 'We will leave in about twenty minutes.' He spoke with the firm voice of one who is accustomed to giving orders.

'Very well.' She lifted her table-napkin from her lap and placed it on the table.

She found herself enjoying the speed of his driving on the way to the laboratory.

'I got my first glimpse of all the sugar-cane on the island from the plane,' she said. 'In fact, I was terrified. It seemed to be rushing up to meet us as we prepared to land.'

He turned to look at her. 'So you were nervous? Well, it is a rare woman who approaches anything objectively . . . even an airport. Everything that happens to her, no matter how trivial, is an emotional experience.'

'I don't see it that way.' Her voice was stiff.

'We are approaching the Experimental Station,' he told her. 'You will work in the laboratory in this building.'

Glancing about her, Meredith said, 'I see. And those houses over there—was I supposed to live in one of them with Gérard Catroux?'

'Yes, you were.'

'How am I to get here every day? I mean, although it's on the estate it's some distance from your house.'

'I intend putting a small car at your disposal.'

'I see. I've really started something, haven't I, by not being a man?' She lifted one hand to the nape of her neck, beneath her tawny-blonde hair, and her green eyes were troubled.

'Don't worry about it.' He spoke carelessly. 'I intend making the best of my dilemma.' He bent over to undo the door catch for her and she saw his eyes travel down her legs, and her senses vibrated when he touched her.

As they walked in the direction of the white building he said, 'Here, scientists investigate all aspects of sugar-cane agriculture. The main functions of the Station are to develop new varieties of sugar-cane, study soil types and to eradicate pests and diseases and to provide information relating to cane production. There is also a plant-breeding section of the Experimental Station, where thousands of seedlings are cultivated yearly. We also run an experimental farm, nearby.'

The laboratory in which she was to work was bright and sparkled with demijohns, bottles, tubes and the kind of lipped glass beakers used for scientific experiments.

While she was being shown around and introduced to people Meredith almost forgot the real reason why she was on the island.

'And now,' Marc was saying beside her, 'allow me to introduce Gérard Catroux.'

'We all expected you to be a young man.' Gérard Catroux spoke with a strong French inflection. 'We all understood that you were to share my house with me. . . .' He laughed and his almost black eyes went over her, and she found herself resenting the speculation in their expression.

'It will be more convenient for Miss Cotswold to stay at my house,' Marc cut in easily. 'There was a misunderstanding, let us say. As you can see, Gérard, Meredith W. Cotswold is all woman. Very much so. However, my housekeeper will keep an eye on her— and on me, I have no doubt.'

There remained one more person to be introduced to and that person happened to be a most devastatingly beautiful girl by the name of Chantal Dérain, who had an office to herself. At the sight of her, Meredith's heart contracted with something akin to jealousy. When she found herself alone with Chantal the dark-eyed girl surprised her by getting straight to the point.

'We all expected a young man,' she said, her eyes going over Meredith. 'You know, you are going to make a lot of girls' mammas mad—and a lot of girls! You see, Marc de Chavagneux is something like being on the list of the island's most wanted men. He is wanted, that is, at any chic Mauritius social function. His name is synonymous with 'top-drawer' and top success. Yes, you are going to be hated by many girls, I'm afraid.'

'Are you—one of those girls?' Meredith found herself resenting the other girl's remark.

'But of course. However, he is a mystery man.' Chantal sighed. 'There is murmur, murmur, you understand, of a girl ... Switzerland, I believe. Something. But who knows?' She lifted her shoulders. 'All we know is that he remains aloof, this one.'

CHAPTER THREE

A WEEK later Marc de Chavagneux commented, 'You appear to like your work.'

Meredith had just driven back to the plantation house in the small car which had been placed at her disposal. She was wearing white slacks and top. A vivid floral scarf, topped by a chic straw hat, gave her the artificial smartness of a fashion model. Huge sunglasses covered half her face.

Before she had time to reply his eyes went over her. 'I like it,' he said. 'The chic beyond chic. You have the ability to surprise me constantly, do you know that?'

'To answer your remark—yes, I do like my work,' she replied, preparing to go into the house.

'Good.' His eyes went over her again. 'That is something, anyway.' He settled himself in the Indian straw chair and swung a leg over the arm. 'Part of living for me is to be comfortable at the end of a long, tiring day.'

'I can see that.'

He was wearing belted denims and a dark blue and white striped T-shirt. 'Let me offer you a drink,' he said.

Moodily, Meredith watched him as he mixed a cocktail for her and poured something over ice for himself. Her eyes travelled over him, because he was not looking at her. The turquoise and silver Navajo belt he was wearing with his denims emphasised his lean strength and the T-shirt drew attention to the dark hairs on his arm and again at his throat.

'Like a haunting melody,' he went on, 'you have been at the back of my mind, but that is only because I have known what it is to have held you in my arms and to have kissed you.' He swung round suddenly and she dropped her eyelashes.

In a stiff little voice she said, 'Things have changed since then.'

He passed her the glass which was lightly coated with sugar.

'And I would like to change *that*.' He watched her with lazy interest.

'Of that there's no hope,' she replied quickly, but she felt a shock of excitement.

'We will start with showing you Mauritius, starting with dinner in Port Louis. Everybody has dinner in Port Louis when they visit the island.'

'I would like to point out that you are my employer, Monsieur de Chavagneux.'

'Knowing when to *forget* this is what concerns me.' He sat down again and she watched him swing his leg over the arm of the chair again and settle himself. He went on looking at her. 'Tell me,' he said, 'why did you leave your last employment? I remember you showed great interest in the sugar farmers of this island. There is a man in your life, maybe? A sugar planter?'

'I don't think it's any concern of yours. I want to be . . . courteous with you, but it isn't easy.'

'No?' He narrowed his dark eyes.

'If I'm to remain here may we talk about something else?' she asked. Her voice was stiff.

'Go ahead.' He was smiling now.

'Well,' she shrugged and looked around, 'do you own all this land? All these fields of cane?'

'While I am not listed on *Fortune* magazine's list of millionaires. I am not exactly a poor man. So?' He gazed past the veranda. 'You are impressed?'

'I didn't say I was impressed,' she answered. 'Interested, that's all.'

'Is there something you wish to know?'

'What, for instance?' Her eyes widened. 'I'm simply making conversation.'

'So you are a dedicated conversationalist? I did not know this. But then you are intriguing, fascinating and exasperating. This I do know.' Was there a suggestion of moody calculation in those dark, tawny-flecked eyes?

'There's nothing intriguing about me.'

'No? Nevertheless, you are a mystery. A mirage, if you like, but no matter, a mirage creates the most fantastic optical illusions. And so far as mystery is concerned, I enjoy solving a mystery.'

Meredith took a sip of her drink and the ice-cubes slid forward, touching her lips. They felt cold, but not as chilled as she was feeling right at this moment.

'I don't know if you are aware—but I have a brother on the island,' Marc said.

After a sickening moment she said, 'I—didn't know.'

'But yes. In fact, he did the job you are doing now—in the laboratory. He is a chemist.'

'Has he—branched out on his own, then? I mean, has he bought another estate?'

'No, no. He is working elsewhere, at present, on another part of the island.' He cupped his chin with his hand and began rubbing it. 'Tell me,' he took his hand away, 'do you like children?'

Her nerves were shrieking now. 'Well, yes. So he has children?' She realised that she was smiling tightly. 'How many?'

'Only one.'

'A little boy?' She was on very shaky ground now, and she knew it.

'A little girl. She is two years old.'

'I see. And so you're the uncle of a little girl?' She took another sip of her drink. 'How nice. Does she have a French name? She must do, of course.'

'Are you really interested, or are you just making conversation again?'

'You can be very insulting,' she said, biting her lip

and turning away from him.

'Colette was born out of wedlock, as they say,' he went on. 'She is being brought up by a French nurse. Elderly, strict ... but she knows what she is about. She is excellent with children, I believe.'

'Well, that's always something. What's she like, this little girl?'

He shrugged. 'Oh ...' he appeared to be thinking about this, 'a parcel of energy, of that there is no doubt. A volatile, often precocious child and, it must be admitted, on occasions, a great responsibility on my brother. Often, though, she is very subdued.'

Without thinking Meredith said, 'That will be because she's missing her mother.'

'Now why do you say that?' He shifted his position and gave her a sudden hard glance. Or was she imagining it? A shock ran across her nerves.

'I merely put two and two together. I mean ... the nurse, and everything.' She felt like taking to the cane in the distance.

'I must take you to visit them,' he said. 'You would also, I believe, enjoy to see my beach house. It is really very beautiful. There is a pool.'

'You're very fortunate, aren't you? All this,' she lifted a hand, 'and a beautiful beach house with a pool.'

'It is interesting to speculate whether I am fortunate or not. These things are not complete without a beautiful woman. But yes, I suppose I am fortunate in that I like living with my favourite things, make no mistake.'

'And I suppose that means living with your favourite women?' she could not resist saying. 'I think—if you'll excuse me. . . .' She set her glass down on the plate-glass table top.

Dining with Marc, with only the coming and going of the housekeeper, was a strain. Candles flickered in Tiffany vermeil palm-tree candlesticks and the table gleamed and glinted with Tiffany silver and French crystal. In the soft glow Marc's skin appeared darker than usual and his dark eyes caught little flares of candlelight.

'Why are you so tense?' he asked, when they were alone. 'Is it because you have known what it is to have been in my arms, to have known what it is like to be desired by me and to have *shared* that desire?'

'I don't have to sit and listen to this!' she said angrily. 'Please explain to your housekeeper, when she returns, that I'm not hungry which is perfectly true, really.'

'Ah, so you have become a stickler for the truth, Meredith?' He smiled at her and his dark eyes followed her as she left the room.

She found, later, that she was tired but in no mood for sleep and it was long after midnight when she decided to get out of bed. Opening the French doors, she stepped out on the long upstairs veranda to gaze at the night under Mauritian stars. On either side of the drive the palms appeared almost silver in the light from the moon.

She would have to get in touch with Richard Parker, she found herself thinking for the umpteenth time, because she could not go on with this. Perhaps she could get out of this crazy situation before Marc found out why she was here in Mauritius?

'Do you know something? I would like you to dance for me, swathed in nothing but gauzy veils.'

At the sound of Marc's voice, she swung round.

He went on, 'You look like a windswept goddess. Why do you look so startled? My door, and others, all lead on to this veranda. That is what it is for—people come out here when they cannot sleep. Why is it that you cannot sleep?' His dark eyes went over her. 'I like it—your nightdress—it is a composition of dreamlike mystery. You know . . .revealing surprise at every turn, for you must realise, of course, that it is breathtakingly transparent.'

'I couldn't sleep,' she replied. 'I didn't expect company.' She was resolved not to give herself away but, at the sight of him, a feeling of excitement had taken hold of her.

He came over to where she was standing. He was wearing nothing but a pair of heavy silk sleeping shorts and, in the light coming from the moon, they appeared a deep ruby red.

'Why is it that you could not sleep?' he asked.

'Because it's hot, I suppose.' She gathered the folds of her nightdress between her fingers in an effort to screen her nakedness from his appraising eyes.

'Here, seasons only exist in the calendar,' he replied. 'Summer never dies.'

Meredith moved away from him, experiencing a curious sensation of almost hostility towards him, mingled with danger and excitement. 'I was just leaving, anyway,' she told him.

'Don't change your mind.' He caught her by the shoulders and looked down into her face. His eyes travelled down to her throat and back to her mouth.

'I don't know what you're talking about,' she said. 'What do you mean?'

'I mean—perhaps it was your intention that I should find you here?' The tone of his voice was taunting. His arms closed about her as his lips sought her own. It was a strange, timeless sensation while all the feelings she was experiencing were concentrated on her lips, before taking command of the entire length of her. She clung to him, then, feeling a premonition of the excitement she would experience with Marc de Chavagneux, because that time *must* come. Not now, maybe, for she was not ready to give herself to him ... but the time would become ripe.

Coming to her senses suddenly, she struggled against the swimming of her senses, but Marc held her tight against him and she found herself discovering the

impulses of her excited body—and his—and she realised that she was facing something completely beyond
the limits of her experience with men. Against her lips,
Marc groaned softly. It was a sound of despair, almost,
and it had the power to terrify her, switching her off,
almost.

'Stop it!' she begged, moving her head from side to
side.

'No . . .'

'Let go of me! What do you want me to *do*—have
hysterics?' She fought him off. 'I don't want you to—
touch me,' she panted. 'If you come near me again, I'll
scream my head off!' She backed away from him.

'You do not expect me to believe that?' His breath
was a little uneven.

'I do. I would have been better off staying in the
house with Gérard Catroux. I'm—I'm afraid of you.'

'If you are, it is because you are basically afraid of
yourself.' There was a gleam of anger in his eyes. 'Go
back to bed. You are both beautiful and maddening.'

'More reliable judges than you have told me that
I'm beautiful,' she said. 'It doesn't excite me very
much, actually.'

'No?' He laughed softly, but made no attempt to
stop her from leaving.

She awoke to the brush, brush of those sweeping
brooms and the sprinkling water noises in the garden,
as women with floppy straw hats and wearing bright
colourful saris swept the lawns and walkways, brushing
away fallen hibiscus and papery bougainvillea petals.

Cool and stylish, she left the house without seeing
Marc and drove to the laboratory.

Later in the day, a reckless streak in her caused her
to accept an invitation from Gérard Catroux to drive
to a hotel for cocktails after work.

In the car, beside Gérard, and again at the open-air
lounge at the hotel, she tried to let the magic of the

island wash over her, but she felt tense. Her thoughts revolved around Richard Parker and his grandchild, Colette, and the part she herself was playing in getting Colette back to her young mother. Into the bargain, she was quite aware of the fact that Gérard was, in fact, everything Marc had hinted at.

Refusing a second drink, she said, 'Gerard, I really must get back to the estate now.'

'Oh, come on,' his black eyes went over her. 'Why?'

'I have things to do,' she replied.

'He doesn't possess you, just because you happen to be staying at his house, surely?'

'Of course not. It's not that.' She shrugged.

They drove back to the estate in a huffy silence, but after a while, Gérard took her hand. 'Come,' he said. 'I'm jealous, but is it a crime to be jealous?'

The touch of his fingers sent a shock of revulsion along her nerves. She did not want to be touched by him, and she took her hand away.

Marc was on the veranda and his deliberate tawny-flecked eyes took Meredith in from head to toe, without appearing to do so, as she came up the steps with Gérard.

'We have been gadding,' Gérard said easily, 'as you can see,' and because she did not know how to cope Meredith went straight into the house.

Marc was not present at dinner and she did not see him until the following afternoon, when he surprised her by suggesting that they should drive out to his brother's house on another part of the island.

'That would be very nice,' she answered, feeling like a traitor. 'I—I'd like that.'

'You would?'

'Yes.' She tried to smile, but she was thinking about her last letter to Richard Parker, in which she had mentioned that André de Chavagneux did not appear to be taking an active rôle in matters concerning the estate and that, up until the moment of writing, she had made no progress whatsoever in coming into contact with Wayside Flower.

As if reading her mind Marc said, 'You will meet Colette, of course. She will give you something to think about.'

Meredith widened her eyes, but she knew she sounded on edge. 'Why should she?'

'I explained to you, did I not, that she is a parcel of energy.' His voice could not have been more casual.

'Oh, yes, I believe you did. A great responsibility to your brother, I think you said.'

'You have a good memory.'

She was resolved not to give herself away. 'Well, sometimes. . . .'

There was a small silence and then he said, 'By the way, I wish to make it plain that I do not wish to be bombarded with the constant presence of Gérard Catroux in my house.'

'I don't know how you can say that,' she said. 'He doesn't make a point of being here.' Turning her head from him, she felt her cheeks begin to grow hot.

'It is your own affair what you do with him,' his voice was scathing, 'do anything you like, in fact, only count *my house* out.'

Under normal circumstances she would have told him that she had changed her mind about going to his brother's house, but in view of the fact that she had a job of work to do there, she remained silent.

On the way there Marc pointed out a wayside shrine, with a candle burning inside, and at the word wayside her nerves tightened up.

'Mauritius is so *different*,' she tried to speak casually. 'What's more, you must find it very different indeed from Paris. Don't you ever miss Paris?' She turned to look at him.

'I cannot say that I do.' He thought for a moment and then went on, 'In Paris the light is soft somehow, never harsh or strong. The winters, however, are a different. matter, with endless grey and dreary days. Perhaps I miss Paris a little.' He shrugged.

'I should have thought that Rome or New York . . . any big city, for that matter, would have appealed to you more than a little island.' She went on talking to take her mind off Richard Parker, who was waiting for news about little Colette . . . news which she should soon be in a position to give him. She felt suddenly sick with self-hatred.

'At the present time of my life,' Marc was saying, 'a view through trees, across to the Ile Saint-Louis and the comings and goings of river barges on the Seine, as observed from the elaborately-draped windows of an apartment, are not for me. I have lived in such an apartment, of course—for a while.' He was silent for a moment. 'No, I like this island. I am well acquainted with it—the climate, the colourful way of life, the romantic past. For all the problems that face many of the people here, one very lighthearted quality remains vibrantly alive. That quality happens to be a sense of pageantry. You will not have had time to notice this, but many people are poor here, but then many people are poor anywhere, no? They are, perhaps, more than just a little preoccupied with the endless routine of living and 'making do', but they never fail to bring colour and glamour into their lives. You saw, for yourself, the joy of the sega dancing.'

'I was thrilled by it,' she answered, thrilled by being able to talk to him like this.

'So? The people here are not interested in such matters as seeing their names in society columns and, in this respect, they are not missing much.'

He took a hand from the wheel and reached for her fingers, raising her hand until his lips were on it. 'Also, in Mauritius, I can watch the heavenly bodies at night—one in particular in a flimsy nightdress. I must warn you, Meredith, that I am not one to go by the rules, so be careful next time.'

'There won't be a next time,' she replied quickly.

'Unless I read the signs incorrectly, there is some confusion about this in your mind,' he said, and then she could feel his tongue against her skin, giving substance to the words.

Immediately her sensual feelings were roused and she almost stopped breathing, conscious of that tiny, languorous movement going on against the palm of her hand.

'So,' he sounded amused, 'you do not like this—this quickening of the senses?'

Snatching her hand away, she snapped, 'I wish you'd stop it!'

She turned away from him and gazed out of the window. The landscape was picturesque with undulating sugar fields. In places, there were small forests and the strange, almost moonscapish mountain peaks were never very far off. In the distance, beaches were crescent-shaped and the breakers on the reef looked like lace.

'My brother is living in a house, which belongs to the sugar mill where he is employed at the moment,' Marc told her.

'Oh.' Meredith's voice was small and tense.

A middle-aged woman was amusing a small girl on the lawn and, with all nerves beginning to shriek for deliverance, Meredith realised that she was looking at Richard Parker's grandchild Colette.

By the time Marc had parked the car, André de Chavagneux was there to meet them, and Marc made the necessary introductions.

André's eyes were dark and mysterious but, she noticed, lacked those strange tawny flecks which made the eyes of his brother so fascinating. His hair was dark and his face rather long and oval-shaped with what was obviously the de Chavagneux regular features. He appeared slightly younger than Marc, but to have suffered more than his brother.

Directly Colette noticed her father she came forward at a run for him to lift her in his arms which he did, swinging her high above his head. The small girl shrieked with delight.

'What language does she speak?' Meredith asked.

'She's slow at speaking,' André answered. 'But,' he smiled and shrugged, 'a few words of French, a few of English.'

'Well, of course she's young,' she replied, 'and I—I suppose she becomes mixed up.' She shrugged helplessly, afraid to say too much.

'Some children walk earlier than others, some learn to talk earlier,' Marc cut in. 'It will come, won't it, my little ragamuffin?' He ruffled Colette's dark hair.

Leaving Colette with her nurse, André led the way into the house where cane was used as the central furniture theme, creating a relaxed, casual scene.

'What an attractive house,' Meredith told him.

'You must come again. If Marc won't bring you,' he glanced at his brother mockingly, 'you must come alone. Colette sees too much of her nurse ... but,' he lifted his shoulders, 'it is just one of those things.'

Conversation became general and Meredith found herself relaxing, but only slightly.

In the car going back to the estate, Marc said, 'Well, you did very well.'

'How do you mean?'

'I mean Colette appeared to have taken a fancy to you.'

'Just because she asked me to lift her up before we left?' Her voice was tense. Had he guessed?

But no. He looked amused. 'You mentioned that you like children, did you not?'

'Well, yes.'

'So you can drive out to the Mill whenever you wish. It will give you a chance to get away from me, no?'

'There's always that to it.' She tried to keep her voice light.

CHAPTER FOUR

THE days were going by swiftly, and in spite of herself Meredith was enjoying living and working on the beautiful island.

'You know,' Marc said one evening, 'I think you have changed.'

They were dining by candlelight and her green eyes met his over the flickering orange spears. The gleam and glitter of silver and crystal was highlighted by an arrangement of flowers of summertime in shades of pink and scarlet, orange and yellow and blue, seemingly chosen at random but blending beautifully and casually arranged.

'Changed? How have I changed?' Her voice hovered between irritation and defence.

He moved in his chair and sat back and studied her and, watching him, she found herself thinking that he always moved lithely, like a cat, and as always, it excited her.

Beneath the table, with its cloth flouncing to the floor, she swung a gold-sandalled foot and did her best to keep her gaze steady.

'You seem to be losing a certain hardness which I had discovered about you.'

'I was never—*hard*,' she replied swiftly.

'No? Well, that is my opinion.'

She shrugged helplessly. 'Well, you're entitled to your opinion, I guess, but it's what I think of myself that counts. Besides,' her voice was sarcastic, 'this is a flattering hour.'

'This has nothing to do with soft lights and a flattering hour,' he said. He was wearing beige trousers and a beige silk shirt, open at the neck, and it was striking how this subdued tone complemented his almost fierce, dark good looks. A gold locket glinted between the dark hairs on his chest. His sheer physical impact caused her senses to swim. He was a handsome Frenchman who, like his grandfather before him, was wedded to the Mauritian light and natural beauty. Narrowing his eyes appraisingly, he said, very softly, 'You can be frank with me.'

'What do you mean?' Her gaze locked with his.

'Why did you lie to me?'

Her heart did a complete flip. 'What about?'

'Your name. What else?' He leaned back again and regarded her.

'I thought that was over and done with?' she murmured. 'You're no longer Serge Jourdan. I'm not Merry Richmond but Meredith Cotswold, and I'm employed by you as a laboratory assistant.' She felt her confidence dwindling, however.

He went on regarding her and then she heard him sigh impatiently. 'Forget it.' His voice was harsh. 'You have not changed at all. My giddy feelings for a beautiful and desirable little liar were beginning to govern my behaviour. Anyway,' he shoved his chair back and stood up, 'I have work to do. Take your coffee out to the veranda. It is cool there.'

The strain of trying to say and do all the right things began to tell on her, but often she would drive out to André's house, the tiny car completely dwarfed by high sugar cane, at times.

She had grown familiar with the sights of those strange hump-backed cattle drawing carts, piled high with sugar cane, the pyramids of lava caused by volcanic eruptions which dotted the fields, the rugged mountains which form the backbone of the island, and the faces of the people who lived in corrugated iron and wooden houses in the small villages. Always, in the distance, that glorious blue sea which seemed to stretch to the horizon in a circle and vanishing in a haze which could be the very end of the world. When she thought of leaving the island and Marc de Chavagneux, she almost wished it was the end of the world and that she could remain here for ever.

Into the bargain she felt trapped by the fact that little Colette was becoming used to the sight of her and having her round. Because this was expected of her, she was in touch with Richard Parker, setting out, at considerable length, the activities of the child and her nurse. After posting off one of these bulletins she would become deeply depressed and filled with self-loathing.

'You amuse me with your irrational behaviour,' Marc said once. 'Why is it you do not tell me what is bothering you?' She caught her breath as he put his fingers beneath her chin and with his free arm drew her close. 'Is your work too much for you?'

'No. I'm enjoying my work.'

'It is always a mistake to lie to me, Meredith.'

Had he felt that great shiver which had passed through her? she wondered. 'I'm—not lying.'

'No? Well, we shall see.' Before he released her he bent his lips to hers and kept them there a long time, while her senses swam, and then he released her abruptly.

Much to her surprise he began the habit of offering to drive her out to André's house, and it was on one of these occasions that she had nearly stumbled into her first big trap.

She was in Colette's nursery oohing and aahing over a new doll when, on the spur of the moment, she placed her hands on the child's face and said, 'Your grandfather calls you his little wayside flower—do you know that, my sweet? But how could you?' She felt a wave of despair wash over her, and when Marc spoke out of the blue she swung round, her breath catching and dying in her throat. The silver bracelets on her wrist jangled as her fingers flew to her temples.

'You seem to have an appreciation for wayside

flowers,' he said. He smiled faintly.

'Why do you say that?' she smiled back, and then bit her lip. Her heart was hammering.

'Oh,' he shrugged, 'no reason at all, except that I found a note in the garden. I think I have it here . . . ah, yes.'

At the sight of the slip of paper in his hand Meredith's heart seemed to leap right into her mouth. It was the rough draft of a telegram which she had sent off to Richard Parker soon after her first meeting with Colette. How on earth had she lost it? How careless could she get?

Before she could think of something to say he went on, casually enough, 'Actually, that is not correct. I did not find it. One of the gardeners found it, wedged in the thorns of a bougainvillea, and brought it to me. Apparently it had caught in the branches for some time. It has been out in the rain, obviously. It is your writing, no?'

'Yes, but it's not important—merely a rough draft of a telegram which I sent to a friend.'

'I read it, of course, to see what it was all about. You mention that you hoped to have news of your wayside flower in the near future . . . something like that. It is blurred. And now, I caught the words wayside flower and I suddenly remembered. Your friend is a botanist, perhaps?'

Meredith's shrieking nerves felt suddenly tranquillised. 'Yes, she is, actually.' She felt on safer ground now. In any case, she had been careful not to mention names and addresses on the slip of paper. She had merely prepared the message so that when she went the small post office, near to the mill, she would know what to write on the telegram form, without having to waste unnecessary time.

'She?' Marc sounded interested.

'Yes. She is interested in a particular species, coming from the foot of the mountains on the island . . . growing by the wayside. It—it has a fancy name, I believe, but I can't remember it, of course.'

'Have you found it? Perhaps when you have been out with Gérard Catroux—because I realise, of course, that these outings do take place.'

'I haven't been out with Gérard all that much. Sometimes during our lunch period . . .' her voice trailed away. The temptation to weaken and confess everything was overpowering. 'I haven't had time to look for the little flower, as a matter of fact. It's not all that important.'

'And yet you were going to send a telegram about this?' His tone was mocking, but his eyes demanded that she should look at him.

'I promised,' she said. 'As it so happens, I'm—losing interest.'

'But no, you must not lose interest. After all, you promised this friend. You must *make* time. Perhaps you are spending too much time with little Colette? I myself will take you on a search for this wayside flower.' His voice remained level, though the mockery in it was suddenly more pronounced.

'Honestly, it's not all that important.'

'In any case, I should like very much for us to do this. Well, if you are ready we can be on our way. And so,' he gave his attention to Colette, 'this is the new doll?'

Meredith stood watching him as he fussed over his small niece. He was so tanned, so undeniably good-looking. His head was bent over the doll and his dark eyes were fringed with thick black lashes. She was feeling more distressed and unhappy than she had ever felt in her life.

On the way back to the beautiful and gracious house on the estate she found herself in a bleak mood of self-pity and contempt for Richard Parker in involving her in this impossible situation.

'You are so quiet,' Marc cut into her thoughts. 'Are you feeling ill?'

'I don't feel very well,' she said in a small voice. 'I won't have dinner, if you don't mind.' She knew that his dark eyes were probing her, as he turned slightly to look at her.

'I will see to it that you have a bowl of soup and a salad, with cheese, in your room,' he said. 'Would you like that?'

'Yes, very much, thank you.'

She was feeling shattered. What was to be the outcome of this? The day would come when Richard Parker would fly into Mauritius with one thought in mind, and that was to abduct his own grand-child.

What was even more shattering was that, in the days to follow, she could feel a subtle change in Marc de Chavagneux, because his attitude towards her had taken a sudden swing. He seemed almost to be paying amorous court to her, and she knew it was hopeless. In love with him, and longing to be loved by him, she knew that it was hopeless.

'These moods of yours,' he said one day, almost gently, 'are going to have to be controlled, do you know that? I think you must get away from the estate and from the mill from time to time. You do not have to visit Colette so much—she has her nurse. What is it with you, anyway? So, I think we must get you to relax. We will drive to the mountains in search of your way-side flower. You have something to go on to identify this flower?'

'It's—tiny. . . .'

'Yes?'

She bit her lip and went on. 'Frail . . . in hiding.'

'Yes,' he sounded impatient. 'But what colours do these flowers come in?'

'It's a little single-petalled thing. It's a pale, pale pink.'

'We will do our best, of course. Now,' he sounded amused, 'if you had mentioned a butterfly I might have been able to help you, for as you know, I am well acquainted with the butterflies of this island. Tell me, Meredith, why is it that you do not wear this dress with the butterflies?'

'I'd completely forgotten about it,' she lied.

'So, you will wear it this evening, when we get back. You will wear it for me.' He reached for her hand and lifted it to his lips, and she tried to arrange her thoughts as she found herself wading deeper and deeper. Soon she would be out of her depth. Soon she would drown.

On the day they were going to search for the wayside flower Marc arranged for his housekeeper to pack a food hamper, and he had gone to considerable trouble in choosing a suitable wine.

As he held the car door open for her he said, 'You look beautiful, but then you always do. One thing I always notice. . . .'

'What's that?' Meredith looked up at him, lifting her legs into the car as she slipped into the seat.

'Your perfume—fresh and exciting by day, sensuous and mysterious at night. You like perfume, I take it?'

'Very much.' She wished she could feel happier.

She was wearing a glamorous silky-look shift, in colours of melon, peach, lime and vanilla, over narrow slacks, and a linen hat covered her hair.

Getting in beside her, Marc said, 'I am feeling very relaxed today, and prepared to be a good guide. I will point out all the butterflies, dragonflies, birds and wayside flowers.'

'Thank you,' she answered in a quiet, controlled voice.

The road followed the coast, for a while capturing every spectacular view. Lava formations formed small pyramids in the greenery. Marc pointed out the island's famous balancing-ball mountain, the Pieter Both Mountain, which could be seen from almost every part of the island and from far out to sea. Then he took a road which curved and twisted its way up and revealed wonderful vistas of creeper-festooned forest and occasional waterfalls. There were views of the coast and the saltpans and the blue sea. Once he stopped the car and said, 'If you look very carefully you will see, through the haze, the Réunion island. It is one hundred and sixty kilometres away.' Placing an arm about her shoulder, he said, 'Can you make it out?' She was excitingly aware of his nearness.

'I think so,' she murmured, 'but it's very hazy, isn't it?'

'Perhaps you are not looking in the right direction?' He drew her closer. 'You are looking at the bank of clouds, maybe?'

Aching to be kissed by him, she said, 'Yes, I think I *was* looking at the clouds.'

'Over there.' His fingers were on her cheek, guiding her direction.

Unable to speak, Meredith nodded. She held her breath when he turned her face to his own and her green eyes followed his mouth as he bent to kiss her. He brushed her lips lightly with his and she knew that he was waiting for her reaction, but she was determined not to give herself away. What was the use? she thought bitterly.

She was surprised when he drew back and started the car. 'Your friend, of course, is an expert?'

'My—my friend?' Almost stupidly she turned to look at him.

'Yes, your friend. You know, the lady botanist.'

'Oh.' She expelled a breath. 'Oh, yes, she is.'

'She would like to visit Mauritius, perhaps? A friend of yours would always be welcome to stay at the estate, or my beach house, for that matter.'

'That's very kind of you. I'll pass on the message.'

'In any case,' he went on, 'if we find this flower today you must press it between some blotting paper and send it to her in the post.'

'Yes, I'll do that.'

'And you are not familiar with the botanical name of this shy, frail, single-petalled, in-hiding flower?' He was speaking seriously, but with a good degree of humour, and her nerves tensed as she recognised the same words she had used to describe a flower which did not even exist.

'I told you, I've forgotten, Marc.'

'No problem,' he said. 'I enjoy solving problems.'

Perhaps, she thought, she was so strung up that she saw danger in everything he said?

There were giddy gorges and a deep silence. Once they saw some monkeys. Marc stopped the car in a clearing. It was almost eerie, and yet she knew that only a few kilometres away there were sun-splashed white beaches, villages and roadways. Here they seemed quite cut off. The air was cool and fresh, and yet there was humidity.

They had lunch in this cool, mossy clearing where the moss was starred with pale, pale pink flowers.

'There are enough pink flowers here,' he said. 'This is a coincidence, don't you think? But you said that it was a rare, shy flower, did you not?'

'I'm as confused as you are,' she snapped. 'Actually, I'm losing interest in the whole thing. It's—*her* problem, not mine.'

'You are at your most infuriating, do you know that?' His eyes travelled down her body, as he lowered himself beside her. 'Why lose interest?' The intensity of his gaze made her feel slightly drunk and she tingled to her fingertips.

'I don't see why. I've just lost interest, like I said.'

'*Why?*' His dark eyes fenced with hers. When she made no reply he said, 'That presents a teasing question, does it not?'

Suddenly his arms went about her, drawing her close and his fingers went to her hair, meeting behind her head and then they moved upwards through her hair. She was aware of his warm fingers on her scalp and the sensation was enough to cause her to bring her arms up and cling to him. His lips went down on her own and she moaned, very softly.

The silence of the forest engulfed them and she could feel herself drowning in the silence. Against her mouth Marc said, 'I want you so much, don't you understand? Another five minutes of this and I won't hesitate to undress you, Meredith, and make love to you.'

She felt the increasing excitement of desire. At last, she thought a little wildly, she was free. Free to love. For there was no doubt about it, she had met the one man to whom she wanted to give herself. What happened afterwards was of no importance.

Fully aware of his mounting desire, she felt a warmth begin to spread through her limbs and her body, causing her to feel as weak as a kitten, and yet she was able to press even harder against him. She opened her mouth a little more, amazed at herself, and then, unsure of these almost terrifyingly wonderful feelings, she fought the impulse she had to allow him to explore her mouth and she tried to press her lips together. When he forced them apart, brutally, she felt surprise, mingled with shock for a moment, then she responded to the overwhelming excitement which was now flooding her whole being, sweeping her away with Marc.

He began to undo the zip of her shift, then stopped suddenly as the sound of an engine shattered the moment. When it grew louder Marc released her and she realised that he had sworn in French. He rose to his feet with scarcely a visible movement and reached for her hand, pulling her up beside him.

After a few moments a large and ancient car came into view and six Chinese gazed out at them, blank-faced and inscrutable. Meredith's fingers convulsed in Marc's.

'It's all right,' he said.

The car did not stop and, after it had disappeared,

he said, 'This becomes undignified, to stand the chance of being caught like this. I am sorry. And now, reality must be the order of the day, for I am no longer in the mood for conquest and you are in no mood to search for the elusive wayside flower.' Suddenly he smiled. 'There is more romance in my house.'

'I don't think so.' Her breath was coming a little fast. 'You see, Marc, I wouldn't like this to be repeated.'

'I have strong thoughts about that,' he told her. 'It will be repeated, and you know it.'

'I don't ever want you to—touch me again!' She said.

'I will humour you, for the present,' he said. 'Come, let us pack up, but let me say—those are brooding, troubled words. You want it, as much as I do.' He began to get their things together.

'One day,' he said, not looking up, 'we will drive out to my beach house. We can continue our search for your little flower on the way.' She made no reply and he went on. 'It is an exotic house—very romantic. Near the beach, rather than a beach house, if you can understand, but in any case, you will see for yourself.'

'I have no desire to go to your very romantic house with you!'

He straightened. 'No? Well, I think you will.'

'All I want, while I'm working in Mauritius, is a very settled and controlled way of life.' Meredith picked up her linen hat and put it on.

'While you are working in Mauritius? Oh, so you intend to leave, my little wild flower?' He stood looking at her and she noticed that he was very still.

'When—when the time comes, yes. I mean, that stands to reason.'

'Why does it stand to reason?' He did not let up on his scrutiny.

'Mauritius is not my *home*. Everybody goes back home—some time.'

'You mean—when things are over?' he said. 'But perhaps that will not happen. Perhaps I will keep you here as my prisoner. What do you say to that?'

'I don't even think the risks are worth considering.'

'Beyond any doubt, Meredith, they *do* exist.'

She caught her breath as he walked towards her and took her face between his hands, then, raising it up, he kissed her, and this time his lips were harder and more demanding as he staked his claim on her. His arms fastened about her. For a moment she struggled against him, and then she was aware of his mounting excitement and her own response before he dropped his arms to his sides and stepped back from her. She looked at him blankly. 'It was merely a statement of fact,' he said. 'Beyond any doubt, the risks do exist.'

She stood watching him as he put the food basket into the car.

When they got back to the estate the telephone was ringing in Marc's study and as Meredith went towards the staircase she heard him say, 'What can I do for you, Gérard?'

Her troubled heart lurched and she knew it was Gérard Catroux phoning to speak to her.

'She is not here!' Marc was saying. 'So? What is it you were wanting?'

Listening, Meredith ran the tip of her tongue over her lips which suddenly felt dry, like her mouth.

'I can tell you, here and now,' Marc went on, 'that the answer is no. You see, Meredith is dining with *me* this evening. Right?'

Purposely, she remained standing where she was, with one hand on the balustrade, and when he came back into the hallway she said coldly, 'How nice for you. It's a pity I didn't know anything about it. Since when, Marc, am I dining with you?'

'I will not have you seeing too much of this man, who is well known on this island for his behaviour.' His dark eyes glittered.

'Since when do you possess me? I may be working for you, Monsieur de Chavagneux, but I'm not taking orders from you!' She saw the change in his expression and felt an instinctive thrill of fear.

'No? Well, we will see about that.' He ignored her protests. 'But why quarrel? Do you not wish to see Port Louis by night? At night it has a mystery about it.'

He came towards her, and when he kissed her, she eventually found herself giving way to the quick up-thrust of excitement and responded to his lips with what was, for her, unusual abandon.

After a moment Marc held her away from him. His eyes were mocking. 'You will wish to bath and change and, for that matter, so will I. And do me a favour, please. Wear the butterfly dress—for me.'

In view of the fact that she was nothing but a fake and because she realised that, sooner or later, he was going to find out about her, a stubborn streak in her refused to wear the dress, which was patterned with the butterflies and which had set things on this path in the first place. When she went down to join him she was wearing a very simple black silk dress with fuchsia-pink sandals.

His eyes went over her. 'With you, I am always finding things I did not expect. So? What happened to the butterflies?'

'The dress was creased. I couldn't possibly have worn it,' she told him. Lies, lies, lies. Her nerves were screaming the words.

On the drive to Port Louis Meredith allowed the magic of Marc de Chavagneux—and the island—to wash over her.

As they dined on a balcony overlooking bustling Emmanuel Anquetil Street and they had fun while Marc decided on special dishes which were worthy of Paris.

For a time she almost forgot just *why* she had come

to Mauritius, and then she found herself brooding.

'What are you thinking about?' Marc asked, breaking into her thoughts.

She shrugged, 'Nothing really.'

'Perhaps you do not like the food?'

'Of course I like it.' She laughed lightly. 'Can't you *see* that I do?'

His dark eyes went to her plate, 'So?'

'So—what?'

'So you like the food, but there is something on your mind, I think.'

Once again Meredith found herself lying to him. 'It might come as a surprise, but I was thinking about those weird pyramid things one sees all over the island—jutting up from the cane fields.'

'You were thinking of that, while we are dining together in pulsing Port Louis?' His voice was mocking.

'Yes. Why exactly are they there? They look planned—like haystacks.'

'I did not know you were so interested. I thought perhaps you were thinking of that elusive little flower.'

'I'd forgotten about it.' This was only partly true, of course, for her thoughts were never far from Richard Parker and little Colette.

'Well, to answer your question, those mini-pyramids are basalt rocks and, as you noticed, there is an abundance of them. They are heaped into piles and this is to enable the canefields to be ploughed and so on. They are volcanic rocks. I must show you the craters and the crater lakes one day. The island has a volcanic past. Sometimes when I look at you I feel that there is some sort of volcanic eruption going on inside you.'

For one crazy moment she nearly confided in him, then she exclaimed, 'That's nonsense! Don't you know that, to be really exciting, a woman has to pretend to some mystery?'

'And you are pretending to some mystery?' He lifted his thick dark lashes and looked directly at her.

'Don't be silly. Actually, *I'm* being silly now.' She realised that her smile must appear a little fixed.

Marc studied her and then, after a moment, he said, 'Usually I do not trust a person who lies to me, but. . . .'

'You trust *me*?' she cut in lightly and then her teeth went down on her lip as she gazed back at him.

'I did not say that. No, I do not trust you. Let us say that, regrettably maybe, I often prefer shadow to reality. Sometimes I do not wish to see you as you surely are, only the way I like to dream you are.'

'You seem to go through life with complete indifference to people's feelings, don't you?' The hurt she felt was immediate.

'I have no desire to engage in a clash with you,' he said. 'How did this start, anyway?'

'You say the most terrible things to me. Apparently you like nothing better than to—to punish me. That is, of course, a very chauvinistic characteristic.'

'Not at all. As I become older, I become more scrupulous about truth,' he told her.

'And of course, you always go by the rules, don't you?' she replied sarcastically. '*Monsieur Serge Jourdan!*'

'You are wrong,' he told her. 'At the present time there is nothing in the world which interests me so much as your wellbeing. I do not wish to punish you. You are in a bad temper. I brought you here to enjoy yourself, so,' he lifted his glass, 'let us live for the moment.'

'Is it permitted to ask why you say *at the present time* there's nothing in the world which interests you so much as my wellbeing?'

'There is nothing to prevent me from changing my mind,' he replied easily, 'except your deceit.'

'Which is over and *done* with, surely?' Meredith broke off, at a loss. Of course it was not over and done with. It had, in fact, only just begun, so far as Marc was concerned. She dreaded the day when he would discover the full extent of her deceit. Her green eyes, which seemed to be asking for sympathy, were luminous.

For a moment he made no reply and it almost seemed as though he was considering how to deal with her, then he smiled. 'As usual, you are becoming troublesome.' He leaned forward to replenish her wine glass. 'It is a matter of astonishment to me that I put up with you.'

On the drive home she rolled down her window and the breeze blew her hair about her face and gave her a feeling of freedom. That it was false, she preferred not to think about.

The moment Marc opened the huge door she was aware of the feeling of drama and romance. She went with him to the kitchen where they made coffee and carried it back to the lounge.

'You're being very nice to me, for a change,' she commented.

'I am glad you find it so,' he answered casually. 'I advise you very strongly to make the best of it.' He was smiling, however, when he said this but, sensitive as she was about her relationship with him, Meredith thought she could detect a hint of calculation in his dark eyes.

He sat down on one of the sofas and looked at her steadily.

'You make that sound like a threat,' she found herself saying.

'Tell me, Meredith, why should I want to threaten you?' He was leaning back, one arm lying along the top of the sofa.

'I don't know,' she answered, feeling an instinctive thrill of fear.

Directly she finished her coffee she said, 'I really must go. I'll never wake up on time in the morning.'

'If you don't, I will personally awaken you by serving you café au lait and croissants in bed. How would you like that?'

'I don't think it's a very good idea.'

'I think you are afraid of me.' His eyes followed her as she stood up, but he made no attempt to stop her from leaving.

When Meredith left for the laboratory the next morning her tawny blonde hair was drawn back from her face and knotted at the neck and her green eyes were serious, because she fully realised that things were getting out of hand.

Marc was on the veranda. 'Good morning,' he said. 'So you made it?'

'Yes.' She tried to speak lightly. 'And now I'm on my way to my beakers and bottles and pitchers.'

'What time will you be back?'

'Oh,' she shrugged, 'lateish—but in time for dinner, of course. Why do you ask?'

'We will dine together at one of the hotels where the palms and filaos rustle to the sea-breezes.'

'Oh?'

'But yes. Now, tell me why will you be "lateish"?'

'I—er—thought of driving out to see Colette.' She waited for his reaction.

'Tell me, why is it necessary to visit Colette so often?'

'I promised I'd go this afternoon.'

'You know what is happening, don't you?' He watched her with unchanging expression.

'No. What?'

'You run a risk of becoming too involved. I advise you strongly against this. Colette is being well cared for by my brother and by her nurse. She has forgotten all about her mother—and here I use the words without exaggeration.' He stopped talking and watched her with an unchanging expression. 'It is best for you to keep right out of this child's life.'

'André hasn't indicated that I shouldn't visit

Colette.' There was an almost frightened look on her face. 'In fact, he seems to welcome my visits to his child.'

'In other words, you mean to go on visiting her?' His eyes were suddenly hard.

'I'm not trying to take the place of her mother, if that's what you mean, Marc.' She felt so tense she felt physically sick.

'It is always a mistake to beat about the bush with me, Meredith,' he snapped. As usual, there was an arrogance about him, an aristocratic air of authority which made the word bush sound ridiculous, and because she felt almost hysterical from nerves, she laughed.

'What is it? Why do you laugh?' Suddenly he came towards her and placed his arms on her shoulders. 'If you know what is good for you, you will stop seeing this child so often.' He was full of impatience and his tone did not invite argument.

CHAPTER FIVE

HONEY-SKINNED and aware of her body and the feelings which Marc de Chavagneux was arousing in her, Meredith gave way to living only for the day. That she was distrustful of the future, she tried not to think about, and all she wanted to do was to be with the man she loved. There were days, however, when she was acutely depressed and withdrawn, mostly after she had posted a letter to Richard Parker, setting out the daily routine of Colette and her French nurse.

Often she was tempted to lift the telephone in her bedroom at the estate and dial Richard's number in South Africa and make it clear to him that she could not continue with this strange commission.

When she was with Marc, however, her senses swam, and it was a matter of indifference to what the future was holding for her. After work and during weekends Marc showed her the island, taking her to Chinese restaurants and lively night clubs and a hotel which had a reputation for wonderful Indian food.

Once she tried to draw him out about the women in his life, and there had been a perceptible hardening in the expression of his dark eyes. 'There have been women, certainly, but I am too much of an expert, Meredith, to be caught in anyone's web. But why ask? Surely you do not believe that I would be fool enough to tell you?'

They were lying on a beach one day, when Marc caught her unawares by saying, 'What is he like—the man for whom you worked in South Africa?'

She had difficulty in using her voice. 'Well . . . he's a dignified, slightly austere man. He—has a dry sense of humour.'

66

Suddenly, to her surprise, he laughed outright and sat up and looked down at her. He began to brush the pale blonde sea sand from his arms.

'A dry sense of humour?'

'Yes. What's so funny about that?' Her eyes went over his face.

'No, no, it is nothing. The way in which you describe this man—he must be elderly, no?' His eyes travelled down her tanned limbs before he lay down beside her. She was acutely aware of his body next to her own.

'What is this? A cross-examination?' She moved away from him. 'I wasn't in love with him, if that's what you mean.'

Marc began stroking her back and, face downwards now, she closed her eyes, weakening at his touch.

'Maybe I am jealous about this man. But you can be frank with me about this sugar magnate, Meredith. Tell me about him.' His fingers went to her hair and rolling away to one side she squinted at the dazzling sun and looked up at him. Her beautiful face was a sun-bronzed oval of indecision, and it was also slightly pale as she struggled with the temptation of confiding in him.

'There's nothing to tell.'

'No? Are you sure?' Marc went on looking at her, then he sat up and reached for her, drawing her up into a sitting position beside him.

Her green eyes went to his mouth. 'I'm quite sure.'

He drew her close and then downwards until he was leaning over her. She gazed up at him, knowing what she was about to do, then he raised her face slightly to his and kissed her. His expert hands began to fondle her and she felt his excitement and her own mounting response as his lips became harder and more demanding. A delicious warmth spread through her as he allowed her head to sink back on to the warm sand, leaving her peculiarly weak, but not weak enough to prevent her from pressing harder against him. Amazed at herself, she opened her mouth slightly, for she knew what she was about to do here on this very private island beach with its rustling, rattling palms and the thunder of breakers out on the coral reef. Nothing was real, except this moment on a warm, white sickle of sand in the arms of the man she loved.

He drew back and looked down at her. 'That night,' he murmured, 'when I first came upon you on the veranda you looked like some beautiful windswept and wild goddess, do you know that? I could see right through the flimsy garment you were wearing and I wanted you very much . . . very badly.'

When she began to murmur something he kissed her, sealing her lips. 'Don't,' he said, almost impatiently against her mouth. 'Don't say it. Just don't say anything,' then he released her suddenly and she felt a little dazed. There was, she thought in her sudden humiliation, something baffling and confusing about him.

'There's something so—hard—about you,' she said, very softly, her breath coming quickly. 'Sometimes you really shake me. Do you treat other women in this fashion, Marc? For there must be others in your life. Are there?'

'But of course!' His voice was cold, irritated, harsh. It was the voice of a complete stranger. 'Did you expect me to tell you that I have always lived in the cold Spartan cave of a hermit?' His eyes went over her. 'Get your things together. It is more than time to get back.'

He was not present at dinner. Meredith ate alone, then she heard him drive away in his car and became aware of the beginning of a terrible loneliness.

She was in a troubled sleep when the telephone at her bedside rang and she lay listening to it stupidly until she realised what was happening. Although Marc had arranged an extension she had never received any calls. Her heart was racing as she lifted the white receiver. Was it Richard Parker? Had something gone wrong?

Marc's voice answered her. 'Are you awake?'

'Well,' her voice shook, 'what do you think? I'm answering, aren't I?' Her hair cascaded over the pillow as she moved the phone to a more comfortable position. 'Is—something wrong?'

'Nothing is wrong. I want you to pack a bag.' There was a hint of tension behind the words.

Sitting bolt upright, she said, 'Why do you want me to pack a bag?' Her eyes flew to the tiny space beneath the door. 'Is—is the house on fire?'

He laughed softly. 'No, nothing like that. I want to marry you. We will go, first thing in the morning, to Curepipe. I have already made the necessary arrangements. We will then leave for my beach house. You can come back here, later, for more clothes.'

A great tremor passed through Meredith's body and she could think of nothing to say as she tried to take this in.

'Meredith?'

She swallowed. 'Yes?'

'Does this bother you, or do you see yourself married to me?'

'It bothers me very much, but—I want to marry you . . . very much.' She discovered that she was crying silently.

'So? What is stopping you?' He sounded angry.

Her face was half hidden behind her tangled hair and she pushed it back with shaking fingers. 'Oh, don't *ask* me!' Her voice was broken.

'I want to know.' It was a command.

Searching desperately for a way in which to tell him about Richard Parker, she ended by saying lamely, 'It's the question of religion—yours and mine.'

'That is all?'

She went on crying and biting her lips in an effort to keep him from knowing. 'Yes,' she said at length, and thought she could hear him sighing loudly.

'In any case,' he was speaking patiently now, but it sounded as though it was an effort on his part, 'we will be married twice—once in the Town Hall and again in the church, when we have overcome certain obstacles.'

Barely able to speak, Meredith said, 'I'll have to think about it.'

'I must know now. Make up your mind.'

'You *know* I can't!' Filled with a wild and hopeless despair, she was already planning her departure from Mauritius.

'Tell me about it!'

The thought of saying goodbye to him was too much for her and she held the receiver away from her as, with her fingers cupped over her mouth, she wept bitterly, moving her head from side to side.

'Meredith?'

Taking a long recovery breath, she took her fingers away and said into the mouthpiece, 'I'll—marry you.'

She had believed herself to be ruthlessly in control of what she had come here to do—and yet here she was, in love with the only man she could love completely—the brother of the man on whose child she had come to spy with the object of having her snatched from the island.

The sky was powder-blue and shell-pink when she began to pack all her prettiest clothes. Perhaps, after they were married, Marc would forgive her. It was a chance she would have to take, she told herself, especially if she could persuade Richard Parker to leave his grandchild in Mauritius with her father and nurse.

When he tapped at her door she was wearing a white spaghetti-strapped dress, with a black jacket, and she looked at him apprehensively as he came into the room. He looked pale, she thought, and he was not smiling. Coming over to where she was standing, he placed his hands upon her shoulders and looked down into her eyes.

'There were many applicants,' he said softly, 'one of

which was from a very beautiful girl who I believed to be a man and, taking it from there, she has had the ability to surprise me constantly. My waking hours are filled with thoughts of this girl, and so are my dreams.'

Meredith noticed that he did not mention that he was in love with her.

'I half expected you to have gone,' he said.

'I *should* have left here,' she replied quickly, trying to pave the way to tell him what was on her mind.

'So? You were, in fact, contemplating this? Why, Meredith?'

She clung to him suddenly. 'I don't know,' she whispered. 'Don't let's talk about it.'

She had made the transition from what really amounted to being some sort of spy to becoming Mrs Marc de Chavagneux—within an hour, or so—after having written a letter of explanation to Richard Parker, which she still had to find time to post.

After the impersonal ceremony they began the drive to Marc's beach house on another part of the island. On the way there he was unusually quiet, except to point out places of beauty or interest to her. His disinclination to make conversation, however, gave her the necessary time to try and shuffle her thoughts into some kind of order.

The air was cool, humid and fragrant. They passed through the usual villages which were jammed with goats and chickens. Mauritius, she thought idly, was a complex of beauty and ugliness with its straggling settlements and magnificent scenery. The entire reason why she was here was almost unbelievable.

Women wearing colourful saris added colour to the landscape, and sometimes they overtook a cart drawn by hump-backed oxen. Once, to break the silence, she asked, 'What's that man wearing, Marc? In fact, I often notice men dressed that way. Are they—djellabas?'

'I really don't know,' he replied abruptly. 'Since you

are so interested you must ask someone else.'

The tone of his voice had the power to surprise and hurt her, and for a while she sat in a huff, struggling with tears of outrage. She knew perfectly well that she was going to end up, eventually, as the loser, and the thought caused a faint shudder to pass through her.

A mongoose crossed the road and then, a little later, a troupe of Macaque monkeys. Her eyes, green and unhappy, followed the troupe as it disappeared into a clump of traveller's palms.

'And so,' Marc broke into her thoughts, 'slim, glamorous and with careful make-up, you became my wife in the Town Hall in Curepipe?' A mask seemed to have been fitted over his handsome face.

Not sure what to make of him, she said, 'When you put it like that it sounds ... awful and—flat. Marc, you—you seem so strange.' She gave him a distressed, stricken look. The desire to reach out for his hand was almost overpowering.

'And so, to you, I appear strange? How would you explain that?' He glanced at her and she felt a stab of apprehension. However, there seemed to be an air of lazy tolerance about him now and she came to the conclusion that he was teasing her.

After a moment he said, 'I think you will like my house. It is a setting for seduction.'

'Oh?' Her voice was stiff.

'Also, it is one of the most striking homes built along the sea-front in Mauritius. A very light colour, to merge with the beach, it takes on many different hues with the rising and the setting of the sun. In fact, it frequently changes mood.'

'Like its owner,' Meredith ventured to say.

Ignoring her remark, he went on, 'I gave a lot of thought to the site's vulnerability to wind and rain, not to mention gales, of course.'

'So it's safe during a cyclone?'

'Naturally, on the island, we are all under the constant threat of cyclones, but we are always prepared. We have learned a lot from our past.'

Meredith decided to remain silent. She hoped she might be wrong, but she thought she sensed a tightly-leashed anger beneath the surface of his conversation and drew in an agitated little breath. For the rest of the journey she sat in hostile silence beside him.

The design of the house was completely compatible with the setting. Expanses of glass, with the usual tropical shutters, let in the sea-breezes.

It was a tropical house, with deep overhangs and glass walls that slid open to the sun and sea-breezes— an indoor and outdoor house. From all the rooms it was obvious that there would always be the sound of waves on the coral reef, she thought, looking at it.

Parking the car, Marc turned to look at her.

'Do you like what you see?'

'It's beautiful,' she said softly. 'Really beautiful.'

She could feel the weight of his look on her lips and her throat and then her bosom. 'Everything has been prepared for us,' he told her.

'Oh, I see.'

'I have learned one thing about you, Meredith.'

'What's that?' Her eyes were troubled.

'You are beautiful and you are unpredictable. There are times when I can only guess at what you will do. However, one thing I *do* know, and that is that I find you very desirable. You have a beautiful body. I want you very much.'

There was a shocked little silence and then she said in a small voice, 'Sometimes you worry me. Did you merely marry me because you find me unpredictable, desirable and because I have a beautiful body? I find that very disturbing. You see, Marc, no man has ever possessed me, believe it or not. I don't want to be possessed just because of these reasons.'

'So you have never been possessed by a man? Surely it is no pleasure to have a beautiful body which is unpossessed?' When he took her into his arms she remained taut and her eyes searched his questioningly.

'Let's go in,' she said in a small voice, then watched him as he undid the door latch and pushed open the car door and stepped out. Then he came round to her side of the car and opened the door for her.

'Leave the cases,' he said, 'someone will fetch them.'

When they were inside he said, 'You will want to freshen up first, I think.'

Like the stranger she was, she murmured, 'Yes, please,' and then, 'Marc, it's all been so sudden.'

'We'll think about that later,' he said. 'Let me get you settled before you have a drink with me.'

He led her into what could only have been the master suite, and which was simply beautiful. Sliding glass doors opened on to a spacious patio. Meredith's eyes flew to the kingsize bed with its elaborate padded headboard and glazed cotton bedcover to match, in colours of beach-sand, coral and green. 'Neutral sand' carpeting continued through to the luxurious en-suite bathroom, which had a raised bath. Linking the bathroom and bedroom there was a spacious dressing-room. In no way did Marc's house answer to the description 'beach house'.

'When you are ready we will have a drink before lunch,' he was saying.

She dropped her bag on to the bed and turned away, trying to hide the bewilderment which surely must be reflected in her eyes.

'I'll leave you, then,' he said, and before going to splash her face and applying fresh make-up, Meredith went out to the patio and gazed at the view, which was breathtaking. A short distance away a pale blonde beach was being lapped by a turquoise sea. She was trying desperately not to be depressed and to give herself up to the dazzle of sun and colour and those exotic, waving palms, but she was finding it difficult.

She decided to change into a black silk caftan, then

made her way to the walkway, which had sliding doors on both sides, allowing access to the house, via the main entrance from the garage and parking areas. It was, in fact, where they had entered the house, and she stood uncertainly, not knowing quite what to do, till then Marc joined her.

'Ah, you must be feeling more comfortable?'

'Yes.' Somehow, the air was edgy with tension.

He was looking at her intently. 'Something is bothering you?' When she made no reply he said, 'Don't look at me like that, Meredith.'

'There's a sense of ruthlessness about you,' she told him, in a small voice.

'I am only too familiar with that accusation. It is, unfortunately, true.' The expression in his dark eyes underwent a change. 'I *am* ruthless. Accept it.' He moved away. 'Would you like a drink?'

'Yes, very much. It—it's so hot.'

'This is a kind of open-air room,' he told her, leading the way. 'Although there is a bar at one end, it is not a bar in the true sense of the word. It is merely a place in which to sip something cool, after a swim—or before dinner, may be—or lunch.'

'It's very attractive,' she murmured, glancing about the room where, again, the accent was on beach colours and the tiled floor, although elegant, was obviously planned to stand any sand that might be carried in. Local-style cane furniture looked inviting and was cushioned in 'island shades'—sand, turquoise, palm-green. Marc slid back a wide sweep of glass which let in the sea-breezes. Arum lilies and irises were arranged in a vase.

The rhythmic pounding of breakers on the coral reef, the sighing of wind were something completely removed from the rest of the world, somehow.

An elderly Creole woman brought in ice and was introduced to Meredith before leaving the room.

From behind the counter Marc said, 'Make yourself

comfortable,' so she went over to the bar and lifted one slim hip as she hoisted herself on to a stool.

'This is such beautiful wood,' she said, in an attempt to make conversation, and trailing her fingers over the surface. Her nails were long, pink and perfect.

'It is blonde wood—like your hair.' He passed her drink to her and there was the tinkling and rattling of ice-cubes. 'Anyway, that is beside the point, right now. I wish to have some conversation with you.'

The muscles of her stomach contracted and her eyes widened. 'Is—something wrong?'

Turning away from her, Marc busied himself at one of the shelves behind the open doors, and when he turned again suddenly, the ice rattled in no uncertain manner as he put his glass down roughly. The contempt in his dark eyes was so naked that Meredith stared back at him. The tawny flecks which always drew attention to his eyes almost danced with a life of their own.

'When a man's wife is a cheat—what do you think? Of course something is wrong. No more fertile ground for conflict could exist.'

'You've—found out?' her voice was faint. Her mouth was dry.

'Found out? I have known, almost from the beginning. I gave you every chance to come clean with me, as they say. At every turn, every opportunity I have tried to draw you out.' He lifted his glass and took a quick gulp and went on looking at her.

'If you've known almost from the beginning,' Meredith asked, 'why did you marry me?'

'Do you think that I went on seeking your company because I was in love with you? Do you think I asked you to marry me because I am in love with you?' He spoke with deliberate cruelty. He was silent for a moment and then went on in a calmer voice, 'Right from the beginning you deceived me. You deceived the de Chavagneux family. You jeopardised the safety of my brother's small child.'

Her heart felt frozen. 'Why did you marry me?' she asked again. '*Why?*'

'In a case like this,' he said, 'the deciding factor was what I was going to do with you until my brother made the necessary plans for Colette to leave this island. He had already made the decision, some considerable time before you came to Mauritius, to leave the estate to work at a sugar mill on another part of the island. Right from the beginning he felt that your sugar magnate might be troublesome. He left the estate and his position as chemist in our laboratory was filled by you— because, you see, your Mr Richard Parker had found out the position here at the estate. What he had not been able to find out, however, was the whereabouts of André and Colette. *You* agreed to do that for him, no? After counselling with my brother I decided to bring you here—you were to be a prisoner, actually, in my house—until such time as Colette was safely settled in Paris, with my sister.'

'So why did you marry me?' Meredith asked, almost shouting at him. What did she expect him to say? she wondered. That he had fallen in love with her and, once they had this thing out into the open, all would be forgiven and they would live happily ever after?

'I had nothing to lose,' his dark eyes went over her insolently, 'and a whole lot to gain. I was in love with a girl who lost her life in a skiing accident in the Alps— so what have I to lose?'

Meredith's heart seemed to freeze and Chantal Dérain's words came to her mind. 'There is murmur of a girl . . . Switzerland, I believe. He remains aloof, this one.' So that was it. Numb with the pain she was feeling, she stared at him as he splashed more liquid into his glass.

Turning, he went on, 'However, I made the discovery that you hold a great physical attraction for me. I want you very much, and the idea of making you my wife became stronger. After all, most important is knowing your "prisoner" well enough to wait until he or she is ready to make a full confession. But it is obvious to me that you are not going to confess . . . even in bed tonight. The prisoner refuses to talk.' He laughed shortly.

'I'm not your prisoner,' she answered. She had the feeling that she was dying from shame and humiliation, and she found herself shaking uncontrollably.

'You are my wife and you are my prisoner. I am buttressed here by a well-trained staff and I have given instructions that you have been ill and that you are not to leave here. But your contract with this Richard Parker has come to an end. It is over and done with. You are now my wife and I intend to enjoy you. Do I make myself clear?'

Her voice was wild with bitterness. 'And all the time I was visiting Colette, André knew?'

'Most certainly he knew of your deceit. It was arranged between us that upon arrival on this island Richard Parker would find himself in trouble.' His dark eyes seemed to switch back and forth across her pale face. 'Even those plans have been changed now— but more about that later, for this is our wedding day, no?'

'It all seemed reasonable to me. . . .' Meredith started to say, but he cut her short.

'*Why* was it reasonable?' His expression chilled her. 'It was so reasonable that, at a high peak in your career as a laboratory assistant to this sugar magnate, you decided to oblige him, and yourself, no doubt, by coming to the island of Mauritius to act as some sort of spy?'

She stared into his face, and at the moment, it was almost a harsh face, and she found herself at once fascinated and repelled that he was her husband. She felt she hardly knew him.

'I felt it was reasonable,' she said. 'I believed that a

tiny child should be with her mother and so—so, armed with this conviction, I came to Mauritius. I—I wanted to help. . . .'

'And what about my brother? Did you think that you would be helping him when you went about your plans to have his only child kidnapped? As far as I can gather, the mother of this child is a mere child herself, who enjoys chattering about her daydreams on a psychiatric couch, instead of getting on with the job, which, in this instance, is being married to my brother.' She heard the hard anger in his voice.

'I didn't know he'd even asked her.' She stared back at him in bewilderment. 'I thought it was the other way around. . . .' Her head began to swim.

'Do, for God's sake, stop beating about the *bush*!' Marc exclaimed, almost violently. 'Honesty means one thing to me and something quite different to you, it would appear. It's time you began to neaten your life, do you know that?'

Dazedly, she watched him as he refilled their glasses, for, strange as it was, they were both empty, as during this whole hideous scene they had both continued to gulp at their drinks, in an effort to become calm.

'And you believe *you* are going to neaten my life for me?' She was breathing hard. 'You're going to keep me here—and neaten up my life?'

'Yes.'

'You're asking for trouble, simply by keeping me here against my will.'

'So?' he shrugged. 'Any form of trouble *you* can invoke, I am able to deal with—make no mistake about that. This marriage is for good . . . not because I love you, but nevertheless for good. You are disloyal, faithless—wanton, even . . . but you are my wife and you will remain so.'

'Stop saying these awful things to me, Marc! Any more of this would be nothing short of slander You can't say all these things to me and get away with it. I won't allow it!' With a shaking hand Meredith lifted the glass to her lips and there was the faint sound of her teeth rattling against the glass. The sea-breeze blew into the room, blowing the soft silken folds of her lovely caftan about her ankles, but she was unaware of the sheer beauty of everything.

'I must make one thing very clear,' she continued, pronouncing each word very carefully, 'and that is— make no mistake. You see, I can handle myself. You will be married to me in name only. If that glamorous, kingsize bed was intended for both of us, you can begin to make other plans—that's for sure!'

His deliberate dark gaze took her in. 'That is what you believe. When provoked, Meredith, I am quite ruthless. However, perhaps that is your intention—that I should be provoked?'

He came from behind the bar with his lithe tread, and she caught her breath as he removed the glass from her fingers and almost lifted her from the stool—all in one movement.

'Let me give you a word of advice.' His eyes travelled down the length of her. 'I do not like being made a fool of. And there will be no need to tease me. You seem set on overlooking the fact that you are married to me.' His voice was dangerously quiet.

After a moment she managed to say, 'And you seem to overlook the fact that a civil marriage is no more than a—a—pagan formality.'

'If it is, I intend to change the so-called pagan formality in the very near future, when you will undergo certain religious instructions under the tutelage of a priest. We will then, before God, be married again in my church.'

'My, my, my—everything is *my* and *mine* with you, isn't it?' She looked at him with furious green eyes. 'And you only care about what *you* want!'

She was fully aware of the calculated note of sarcasm. 'Let us face facts, you have wants too, don't you,

Meredith? In other words, I am fully aware that I strike more than just a responsive chord in you.'

He forced her face upwards and kissed her, but she remained passive in his arms, while the tears ran down her cheeks.

Against her mouth he was saying, 'You are sunshine and you are shadow. I have always known this, almost from the beginning . . . always a dangerous combination, no? Like sudden rain and lightning.' Suddenly he released her, and she gazed back at him with a child's hurt expression.

'This was a—nothing but a premeditated and coldly calculated attack on me,' she said, shaking her head. 'Why don't you just let Richard Parker come to Mauritius—just so that dialogue might take place?'

'Dialogue? What have we to say to this kidnapper? No, it is out of the question. What has been done is over and done with. I don't want to continue with this scene, Meredith. There can be no greater boredom, I think, than scenes which go on and on. This is one scene that had to take place, however, and it is over.'

He was taller than she remembered. She noticed that his eyes were serious.

'I detest you,' she said, and he gave a resigned shrug.

'So, you detest me! That counts for nothing in my estimation.'

'You're so cold and severe that you remind me of one of the pirates who used to violate this island.'

'That may be, but there is an air of peaceful well-being on the island now, don't forget that. You are now my wife and you will make the best of it and, for a while, the pressures of André and Colette will remain far removed, but I will say this one thing—when your Mr Richard Parker decides to fly to Mauritius to kidnap his grandchild, she will have flown too.'

Because there was nothing else for it Meredith had lunch with him. The meal was simple and casual—

steak which had been barbecued on the terrace, served with potatoes cooked in a microwave oven and served with a crisp green salad.

Marc went out of his way to indicate to the servants that he was very much in love with his wife.

During the meal he told her, 'I built this house here in order that, from time to time, I might be soothed by the senses of unchanging timelessness. Here, Parisian boulevards count for nothing. There are no street numbers, no clogged highways. I am always perfectly happy.'

'Buttressed, as you are, by a well-trained staff,' she answered sarcastically.

'You are a problem,' he said carelessly. 'Do you know that? But no matter. I have always enjoyed solving problems.'

'Since you've revealed to me that you're devoid of any feelings,' she said, 'the only one, Marc, who is going to be hurt is me. Do you know that? It certainly won't be *you* or Richard Parker—and his daughter—and your brother, for that matter!'

Moodily she watched him as he poured more wine. Somehow the ritual suited him and suited the surroundings. The wine sparkled within the crystal, big-leafed tropical plants waved in the sea-breezes and, beyond the garden, was the stillness of the idyllic and intensely private beach, altered only by the sound of waves breaking on the reef.

'Just as soon as I can, I'm going to leave Mauritius,' she said. There was loneliness in the words.

'I have other ideas,' Marc replied coolly.

CHAPTER SIX

MUCH to her relief he left her alone for the rest of the day. Her case had been unpacked and her clothes hung up in the built-in wardrobe. She was filled with rage when she discovered that Marc's belongings were also accommodated in the spacious cupboards and drawers, and she stood for a moment trying to decide what she should do about it. In a fit of despair and disappointment she grabbed a handful of his clothing and went to the door, intending to toss everything out into the corridor, but on second thoughts changed her mind. As she put everything back she found herself crying without sound.

When she had composed herself she decided to go into the garden, or to the beach. Anywhere, except being near to the man she had married.

Feeling selfconscious, she left the room, noticing that all the other bedrooms opened out on to either a patio or balcony and arches framed a spectacular view of the sea.

Her green eyes narrowed moodily when she noticed that Marc was already in the garden and seemed to be making his way to the beach, and so, feeling strange and lost, she wandered into the living-room.

Here priceless Persian rugs and paintings were set off to superb advantage against the neutral basic sand colour. She noticed the sort of possessions which she would have expected of him—an emerald snuff bottle, a jade bird, blue-and-white Chinese jardinières, a magnificent Imari bowl. A feature of the entire house was the light golden woodwork, and to offset it there were touches of turquoise, bronze and honey in the cushions and upholstery. At one end of the room, and following the lines of a large corner window, there was a luxurious seating arrangement, upholstered in beige. Honey-coloured scatter cushions were shown off to advantage and flowers had been carefully arranged. For the honeymooners, she thought bleakly, and consumed by humiliation and despair, she found herself weeping again and fled from the room.

Back in the master suite, she collapsed, face downwards, on the huge bed and gave way to the misery she was feeling, making no attempt to control her chaotic thoughts.

After a while she took a bath in the stunning, carpeted bathroom, and cried again while she lay in the water and the steam slowly clouded the light beige tiles.

There was everything for her personal comfort—French soaps and thick towels, and it seemed to suggest that Marc felt it was expected of him to treat her expensively in return for her favours.

Her teeth were clenched as she stepped from the bath and stood before the mirrors, where she dabbed her face with a herbal skin tonic and applied cream. Reaching for the Chinese satin housecoat which she had bought in Port Louis with Gérard Catroux and which was delicately embroidered with sprays of mauve wisteria and branches of flowering cherry, she slipped into it. Her short gold chain, which she had taken off, had dropped on to the floor and, retrieving it, she fastened it about her neck, then went through to the bedroom.

She caught her breath when she saw Marc standing at the sliding doors leading to the balcony. He turned quickly and she was quick to notice his eyes going over her and experienced an odd sense of danger.

'Is everything to your satisfaction?' he asked. When she made no reply he said, 'Meredith?'

'No, it isn't.' She felt her breath coming fast.

'So?' He lifted his shoulders. 'Why is this?'

'I noticed the glamorous new treatment to this room, of course. Much of the décor seems new . . . that elaborately padded headboard, for instance, the cover to match . . . all so feminine. You prepared for this, didn't you?'

'I made last-minute preparations, yes. It really was rather masculine before. In a bedroom a man should feel enveloped in an extension of the woman he is going to make love to. Therefore it should be very feminine. Make no mistake, a man enjoys making love amidst piles of lace and glossy satin.'

Meredith felt herself shivering again. 'I do not intend sharing this bedroom with you!' She was white with temper. 'Under the circumstances, I do not intend sharing this room with you,' she repeated.

'But I do not understand.' Marc spoke on a note of mockery. 'You are my wife, no?'

'I am *not* your wife!' She tried to pass him, but he moved in front of her, between her and the bathroom door where she had intended locking herself in. His hand shot out and he grasped her wrist as she made a move to get past him.

'You will listen to what I have to say.' His fingers were hard and unyielding. 'You are very much my wife.'

Snatching her hand away, she turned quickly, but he was too quick for her and caught it again. He swung her round to face him, then he let her go and she did not move.

Staring back at him with wide green eyes, she was filled with despair. The flame of anger sputtered and died and she began to cry.

'You are very much my wife,' Marc repeated in a softer tone. He reached out a hand and touched her hair. 'You are like a small girl. Why did you not dry your hair? Here, let me do it for you.' She had tossed a towel over a chair and he picked it up and, before she could stop him, he began to rub her hair. 'I thought I would give you time to settle in,' he went on.

'I'm so impressed,' she answered brokenly, and tried to move away from him. He dropped the towel and caught her to him, and she was aware of her nakedness beneath the black Chinese housecoat.

Very softly he said, 'Do not antagonise me, Meredith. We are going to see a lot of each other from now onwards and I suggest you come to terms with this.' After a moment he said, 'I want you so very much.'

'And that, of course, is the most important thing there is, isn't it?' She swallowed and bit her lip, then went on, 'Please spare me the humiliation of having to share a bedroom with a man I detest.' She gave him a distressed, stricken look. 'I don't want you to touch me. You deliberately tricked me!'

'I find this puzzling. Who are *you* to talk about trickery?' His voice was coldly angry.

'My price is high,' she told him. Everything in her world seemed to be falling apart. 'Like good art, my price is love, not lust.'

'Nevertheless, we can be very happy together,' he answered. 'That is entirely up to you. In certain parts of India, I believe, a bride is wished good fortune and good health. No one ever wishes her happiness—and do you know why? This is supposed to lie in her own hands and to be of her own making. I advise you strongly to think about this.'

Meredith struggled against the swimming of her senses as his hands slid down to her hips and she knew that he was aware that, having just stepped out of a bath, she was wearing nothing beneath the black wisteria-patterned garment.

When he cupped her bosom she felt a quick upthrust of excitement but still she tried to push him away. He put his mouth lightly on hers and, flushed with amorous desire, she moved her mouth against his, her eyes closed.

Suddenly, and unexpectedly, he released her and

surveyed her appraisingly. 'So much for your psychology!' She was immediately humiliated and slapped his cheek. 'Get out of here!' she told him. 'Can't you understand that I don't want you to make love to me?'

'Make no mistake,' he said, 'you are about as lovable as a wildcat, right now. I am in no mood for conquest. It is time for you to prepare for dinner. As a matter of fact, I have a surprise for you.'

'I've had enough surprises for one day. I have no desire for you to surprise me.' Her voice held an anguish that was very real.

'I once told you that I am quite experienced in turning a disastrous situation to my own advantage,' he said. 'This is something you will have to learn—but let me say this one thing. You are my wife and I will expect—let us say—good service from you.'

'How dare you!' Her face was white with temper. 'This marriage was nothing but a coldly calculated and premeditated farce!'

'So you have said before, if I remember correctly. But it *has* taken place, and it exists and it will go on existing.'

'It was a strange way of getting even with me. You have a cold and calculating mind.' She broke off and shook her head slowly. 'I just can't believe it; that you should do something like this to a girl. You have a—a devious mind.'

'So? *I* have a devious mind? Talking about devious ways—I gave you every opportunity to be frank with me about your wayside flower Mafia, or whatever you care to call it, but you chose to remain silent. You decided to play out your role of a cinematic blonde spy. You preferred a double life. First, you were a very demure girl wearing a dress with butterflies on it, and then you were the efficient laboratory assistant . . . but all time what you really were was some sort of spy for a man who is no better than a kidnapper. You depress me.'

He walked away from her and then turned round to face her again. 'But let us put it on record . . . I have desired all these personalities. I still desire you.'

'You *lust* after me, let's face it!' She took a quick breath and held it for a moment before she turned away to hide her tears.

She heard him coming towards her, then he placed his hands on her shoulders and turned her round to face him, and she covered her face with her hands. 'Think about this,' he said, very softly. 'At first sight you appeared as sweet and sincere as a girl selling violets on a street corner. But beneath all this was the mystery which has filled me with—with disgust! I knew there was a mystery, believe me, and I set out to unravel it. The mystery is over. We will not discuss it again. That mystery concerned another person—not my wife!'

'I wonder what your brother must think of you,' Meredith said, from behind her fingers, 'for violating me, even if I was no better than a spy. This fills me with disgust!'

'I think it has probably given him something to think about. It would solve a lot of problems if he did likewise and forced this girl to marry him instead of playing around.'

'Do you know what you remind me of?' Her voice was muffled.

'For sure,' he said, almost carelessly. 'A swash-buckling pirate. You have told me this before, I seem to remember. However, when you have pulled yourself together, you will suitably gown yourself and come out of this room and we will begin our honeymoon.'

'God forbid that we have a honeymoon!' She started weeping again.

'Why cry? You merely wear yourself out,' he said, before leaving the room.

In a fit of rage and despair, mingled with a certain degree of spite, Meredith looked out her black chiffon,

with the drawstring neck and butterflies in shades of
melon and deep emerald, which she decided to wear
with emerald tights. Gold and crystal earrings glistened
in her ears. Her face was carefully made up and she
had applied a more-than-usual application of mascara
and eye-shadow in an effort to hide her tear-damaged
eyes from the servants.

Beneath a star-studded sky there was a sega band by
the pool. Meredith's eyes went to the beautiful white
pavilion featuring elaborately carved white chairs and
divans, brass tables and ornate candlesticks. Glassed-
in arches gave on to the glittering water. The sinuous
beauty of coconut palms was enough to thrill the
senses. In the light from the lanterns pale mauve and
purple bougainvillea proclaimed the supremacy of
colour. Servants bustled around and, automatically,
her eyes searched for guests—but there were none.

For a moment she allowed the wild and haunting
music to wash over her, then she made her way to
where Marc was standing. 'I—I'm ready,' she told
him, 'to dine with you.'

He had his back to her and seemed to be staring out
towards the blackness which was the sea, and for a
moment he did not turn. 'So? You are ready? You are
ready for more scenes, maybe? You have been sharpening your claws, no doubt, while busying yourself
with your toilet?' He spoke with a threatening po-
liteness.

For a long moment there was silence between them.
Dried bougainvillea petals blew about like pale mauve
and purple confetti in the breeze. In the morning
Meredith knew they would be swept up by Indian
women, wearing bright saris and floppy straw hats, and
there would be the brush, brush sounds of those
strange little dried grass brooms as they went to work.

Marc turned. Then he surveyed her with a deep
unfathomable expression. 'Maurice will mix us a cocktail before dinner,' he said. 'Come along.'

'Are we going to be alone—with all this?' she asked. 'Or are you expecting guests?'

'There are to be no guests,' he replied. 'Are you going to have something fancy? A coco loco, maybe, served in a coconut shell and adorned with pink and red hibiscus? A daiquiri in a frost-rimmed glass? Something a little more potent? By the way, the young men you see playing sega music are from a nearby village.'

In her despair Meredith felt almost reckless. 'Will you have Maurice mix me a very strong potion? Something to make me feel wildly glamorous and witty. You know, to suit the occasion.'

'I will have him mix such a drink—but not to make you appear glamorous, because you are always glamorous and, God knows you can be very witty.' His voice was heavy with sarcasm.

There were flaming candles in hurricane glasses flaming on the dining-table, she noticed, as they passed it on their way to the bar, where they sat on high stools, watching Maurice as he mixed their drinks. Smilingly, Meredith accepted the fragile, long-stemmed green and gold glass. Then she sat turning the glass round, between her fingers, as she watched the sega band.

When they were alone, Marc slipped a hand into his pocket and brought out a small leather-bound box.

'For you,' he said. 'From me.'

'You don't have to ply me with gifts, Marc. Please spare me the humiliation.'

'Do not antagonise me, Meredith. Open it, or would you prefer it if I were to open it?'

For a moment she sat trying to arrange her chaotic thoughts, then she took the box from him and opened it, and caught her breath. A coral snake, with vivid emerald eyes and curling up into a magnificent bracelet, stared up at her. For a while neither of them spoke, then she said, very softly. 'It's utterly beautiful.' She sighed and held the box out to him. 'I can't accept it, though.'

'How much more of this nonsense?' His voice was cold and very quiet. She watched him while he removed the bracelet from the box and then he reached for her wrist. She was conscious of his taut, lean movements and felt a premonition of excitement. Never had she felt more unhappy—or more alive. Suddenly, however, a remark which he had once passed flashed through her mind and she snatched her hand away. 'There have been women who have pampered me,' he had said. He had already clasped the bracelet around her wrist and she stared down at it, uncertain what to do, without attracting attention to herself.

'Keep it on,' he said quietly.

The waves out on the coral reef were loud when the band stopped playing for a few moments.

'We are about to watch some sega dancing,' he said.

'Well, it's your night,' she answered in a low voice.

'Sometimes it takes patience to put up with you. Do you know that?

'Marc, why should I submit to this? I'm going to contact my lawyer as soon as possible,' she told him. It was bravado. She did not have a lawyer and she was sure he guessed as much.

At that moment Maurice came back to them and peered goodnaturedly at their glasses. 'Something else?' he asked.

'Yes,' Marc answered. 'The dancing is about to begin, Maurice. Please bring the drinks to that table over there.'

A little later he said, 'A beautiful woman with a smooth superb tan, and who knows how to dress, is enhanced when she sips an elegant drink, with all the island trimmings. I enjoy watching you.'

'You're intolerable,' she muttered.

'On the contrary, I am extremely tolerable.' He gave her a mocking smile. 'You will make some discoveries, in the very near future, I hope, that you will not want to leave Mauritius.'

'With its cycles and its seasons,' she replied in a hard little voice. 'Isn't that what you're always telling me?'

Maurice placed their drinks before them and she adjusted her expression swiftly, smiling radiantly. 'Thank you, Maurice. It looks lovely.'

As Maurice left them Marc said, 'I have a new respect for you. Keep it up, darling.' He bent over and kissed the nape of her neck. 'The locals are delighted when they can join us and dance the sega for us,' he went on as a group of young people, wearing bright and gaudy clothes, prepared to dance.

Presently the air was filled with calypso-style and rhythmical pulsating music played by the simple instruments which included a percussion piece called the maracas, a tambourine-like goatskin drum known as the ravane, and the triangle.

'The dance which you will see performed dates back to the times of slavery,' he told Meredith.

'Are you having it performed because you think I'm going to be your slave?' she asked.

Obviously it was a cry from deep within the soul and one which tried to transcend the miseries and heartaches of life, while at the same time expressing a desire for joy and happiness. The beat grew in intensity and the dancing incorporated the beat of the calypso, rock and roll, the twist, hula-hula and Indian folk dancing in a rhythmic, throbbing and erotic display of high spirits.

Meredith's thoughts kept straying. In the morning, she thought, a little wildly, when she awoke to this luxuriant strip of tropical coastline, it would still be as Marc's wife . . . even though she was going to resist sharing his bed.

Suddenly he took her hand. 'What are you thinking about?'

'What do *you* think? I'm thinking about us.' Her

eyes, in the light coming from the lanterns and flaming torches, were green and stormy. 'From where I'm sitting now, I can see the flickering light softening your face, but I know how hard you are. There's nothing soft about you, Marc.'

For a moment he looked at her in contemplative silence.

'Maybe there is something in what you say. However, there are compensations for you. I can be very gentle. This you will discover for yourself.'

A Creole girl brought French and Chinese hors d'oeuvres to the table. 'These are very good,' she told them, smiling.

After she had gone Marc said, 'It should be a very stimulating process, Meredith, have you thought of that?' He settled himself and looked at her.

'What should be?' Their eyes locked.

'Starting from the ground up, as they say. Do you not think? I have also got to know a lot about you, make no mistake. You are like a sun-kissed, swan-necked maiden, with your downcast eyes, sometimes, but I know that you are often unpredictable. In your own way, you are a remarkable girl. However, I advise you not to lash out on our wedding night. Make the most of this night, for you will only be married once— and, here, the word is used without exaggeration.'

Meredith was aware of every small movement he made in the chair so near to her own, and she was perfectly aware of the graceful animal strength in him. She had never in her life met anyone who so totally unnerved her. Just being aware of his movements aroused her sensual feelings.

With languorous, glistening eyes she turned slightly so that she could study him secretly, but he seemed suddenly to have forgotten her existence and was watching the dancers with an almost brooding expression on his face.

Perhaps the cocktails were going to work on her, but

she began to feel an almost delicious feeling of languor spreading over her. During one stage of her adolescent years she had thought it very smart to say to her friends that she was as fatalistic as an Oriental. Perhaps, however, it was fate that she now found herself in this strange position of being married to the dark and handsome Marc de Chavagneux.

When he reached for her hand, she made no attempt to snatch it away, and he turned to look at her. There flowed between them the current of a vague and subtle sentiment which establishes itself between a man and woman on their wedding night. On her wrist, the green emerald eyes of the coral snake bracelet winked in the night.

They dined, and, during this period, the small band changed to slow, sentimental music.

Marc was pointedly attentive to his bride, and sometimes, after speaking to those in attendance, he would laugh, and Meredith discovered that he had a wonderful laugh, happy and infectious. She pulled herself up shortly. If she got thrown by these endearing things about him she could find herself weakening towards him, loving him the way she did. Everything seemed so unreal, and she kept glancing at him with a disbelieving expression. Once, he turned, catching her unawares, their eyes met and clung together, and the sensation was nothing short of riveting.

Pulling herself together, she took a sip of her drink and looked slowly round, taking stock of everything. To break the sensation she said, 'You really must be very wealthy, Marc ... all this, and an island, too. I mean, here, this island might just as well belong to you.'

'That is another compensation for you,' he replied easily. 'I *am* wealthy.' His eyes were suddenly hard. 'So? You have an appreciation for money?'

'Money makes no difference to me,' she said quickly. 'I—I've never been interested in money.'

'No?' His dark, tawny-flecked eyes went on regarding her. 'Sometimes I wonder.'

'What makes you wonder?' she asked furiously.

'I suppose he paid you well to come here—this Parker man?'

'I thought we were to forget that?'

'Of course.' He inclined his head. 'My apologies.'

The meal had been superbly prepared ... salads in stemmed crystal goblets, a casserole in cognac and bananas flambéd in rum. There were Chinese gold-lacquered plates, crystal stemware and Brussels lace on the table.

'The meal was superb,' Meredith felt compelled to say.

'Then I have achieved something,' he replied.

The servants were clearing things away. The sega band had bade them goodnight and the thunder of the waves out on the coral reef was loud and clear.

Meredith stood up. 'Don't let me down, Marc,' she whispered, as he got to his feet and came to stand beside her. 'I don't want to sleep with you. Can't you understand how humiliated I am?'

His face was drawn in a thoughtful mood, and then he said, 'Don't push me to the limit. You are all girl, all woman ... you are my wife. You excite me. What do you expect me to do?'

'You tricked me,' she protested. 'You tricked me!'

'No, I did not trick you. You were eager to marry me—for better, for worse, no? I have absolutely no desire to engage in an act of violation with you. I could label this, but I won't, and I think you understand.'

'But let's label it,' she answered, in a harsh little voice. 'Let's just label it rape, Marc, because that's what it will amount to, if you have anything to do with me.'

Suddenly she turned and ran from him and made her way to the beautiful bedroom, but before she could close and lock the door, he was there. He came into the room and closed and locked it for her.

'In choosing a husband,' he said, 'the heart should rule the head, I should imagine, no? With complete disregard for the chain of events which you have set into motion in the lives of André, his child and myself . . . not to mention the lives of your sugar magnate and his wayward daughter, you allowed your heart to rule your head, and here you are. You are my wife, and I advise you to face up to the fact.'

He reached for her and she almost hissed, 'Don't touch me!'

However, he put both his arms around her and his hold tightened, crushing her body against his own. 'I want you so very much,' he said. 'Can't you see that?'

Hoping to get somewhere with him, she said, 'I'm not prepared to—to be hurried.'

'Right now, I do not care about anything except making love to you,' he told her. 'Beyond any doubt, Meredith, I want you.'

She began to fight him, and for a few moments he held her fast before pushing her away from him.

'There are better ways to amuse oneself than to make love to a deceitful wildcat, I should imagine. I find, after all, that I am in no mood to fight you. You are young—maybe you will improve. Let us hope, for your sake, that you do.'

After he had gone Meredith threw herself down on the bed and wept, then, when she was calm, she washed and creamed her face and slipped into a nightdress, got into the huge bed and turned out the lamps.

In the morning she awoke to windows shaded by gay striped awnings and a balcony which was open to the sea-breezes. For her, this moment of waking was a moment of unreality.

The sheets on the bed felt like silk. Marc had thought of everything, she mused.

A maid tapped on the door and brought coffee and croissants to the bedside. Her brown eyes were expressionless even though she smiled as she said good morning.

When Marc knocked and entered the room Meredith met his glance with a wide stare.

'Today, we try again,' he said quietly. 'From scratch.' He came over to the bed and bent down and put his lips on her own.

After a moment he said, 'You do not answer?'

It was, she thought, useless to argue. 'Yes.' The word came out in a whisper. She was sitting up and bent her head, then she noticed the coral bracelet which she had forgotten to take off, and she felt him watching her.

He was wearing a half-buttoned blue shirt and swimming trunks. His legs were tanned and strong, with dark hairs on them, and she tried not to look at them.

'When you are ready,' he told her, 'we will breakfast beside the pool.' He had a voice of command.

'I thought *this* was breakfast,' she murmured, glancing at the croissants at the bedside.

'But no. Eat what you want and leave the rest.' He still held her eyes with his.

From the windows and balcony there was a view of a beach that looked like a setting for a pirate movie. There were soft drawling Creole voices in the garden and the swish, swish of brushes.

'Today,' Marc went on, 'we will eat and laze and swim.' The silence in the room stretched between them. 'We will stimulate the senses—just by being alive.'

'Yes,' she said again, and there was sadness on her face.

'Most important, we will not quarrel, Meredith.'

She chose to ignore him and watched him as he left the room, then she slipped from between the sheets and went to shower, allowing the water to cascade over her body for a long time.

They sat at a table draped with a vibrant linen cloth and bright with Imari plates and garden glowers, and they were surrounded by flowers in the garden and bougainvillea hanging from a pergola. Scarlet, pink, yellow and white hibiscus added to the beauty in this area of the garden which was screened by white latticework, set up to form a niche. Meredith sat under a straw hat and her eyes behind huge sunglasses were moody and even more green than usual. She wore a floral organdie caftan over a black bikini.

Glancing down at the bowl of chilled melon which had been set down before her, she said, 'My people will be concerned about me. I was rash enough not to mention this m-marriage, but when my letters stop reaching them, Marc, they'll naturally worry.'

Her moody eyes followed his movements as he chose to ignore the melon and helped himself, instead, to a specially prepared baby pineapple.

'I have already gone into that,' he did not look up. 'Except for an uncle and some cousins, with whom you are not in constant touch, you are alone. So?' He lifted his thick lashes and gave her a level look. 'Who is there to testify to your identity? Who is there to care now? If you are honest, you will agree that *I* am the most important person in your life. I am here to care about you—what happens to you. I am right, am I not? I think you will agree—if you have any honesty left in you at all. And by the way, I will be the first to admit that your sugar magnate will have cause, on the other hand, to worry when the Wayside Flower reports fail to come in. So, Meredith, do me a favour, please. Keep quiet about these useless things.'

'You have been busy, haven't you?' She spoke in a tight, bitter voice. 'Quite a detective, in fact!'

'For sure,' he gave her a long leisurely look. 'For sure. East your melon, Meredith, and stop sharpening your claws.'

The house was built above the curve of a white sickle

of sand. There were straw-thatched umbrellas on the lawn just above the beach. A tall, white-domed bird-cage was perched on the edge of the sparkling swimming-pool, looking like white filigree work. Two colourful birds sang inside it.

No expense had been spared, and Meredith found herself marvelling that this wealthy Frenchman was her husband, because he was a stranger to her. Correctly, she estimated that Marc's estate manager must be in complete control, since Marc was apparently relaxing here with no problems.

Women wearing the usual straw hats and bright saris were tending the garden.

'Whenever I am here,' Marc said casually, 'I find myself comparing this lush tropical beauty to the almost ethereal plane and chestnut trees in the boulevards of Paris.'

'Really?' She did her best to appear aloof and withdrawn, but with all that sun and dazzle and the surf pounding against the coral crenellations it was becoming more and more difficult. Marc's strange and exciting eyes kept flickering over her, missing nothing.

When breakfast was over he suggested a walk along the beach, to be followed by a swim. His eyes went over her caftan. 'Take off your caftan,' he said and, almost like a child, she obeyed him.

As they walked along the beach she knew that she loved this island with its white-gold beaches and strangely-shaped mountains, and she found herself relaxing just a little.

Later she lay, near-naked and immobile, tempting the sun to burn her but the coppery tint on her skin only deepened. All the time she could feel Marc's dark eyes on her and the desire within her kept mounting as her body responded to the thoughts which were flashing through her mind. Long-legged and slender, she moved about restlessly, as she pretended to make herself more comfortable. Why not give in, she thought, and forget her humiliation? Why not accept this strange marriage and accept what he had to give and, what was more important, seemed content to give?

She held her breath as Marc moved imperceptibly closer to her, so that their faces almost touched. Dark-complexioned, lean and exciting—the desire she felt to touch him was almost irresistible. Suddenly she found herself in his arms, with no clear idea as to how she had got there. Her small breasts were stretched taut, awaiting their first ripening. His arms tightened about her and she began, very slowly, and then very quickly, to drown. When he removed her bikini top and her breasts were free to the sun and the sea-breezes and to his lips, she bit her own lip to stop herself from crying out.

'Marc, I . . . I don't. . . .' she began, but he cut her short.

'I don't require a speech,' he told her shortly, and the warm, silken firmness of her breast surged to meet his tanned fingers. She heard him groan softly.

He released her, quite suddenly, and sat up, and she lay looking at him, with her breath coming fast and her green eyes wide and bewildered.

Without looking at her he said, 'Let us just say that I have just given you something to think about.'

For a while, neither of them spoke, then she began to cry softly, turning over so that she lay on her stomach, her small breasts buried in the fine beach sand.

'Perhaps now,' she heard him say, 'you will have some indication as to how I felt last night.'

'I didn't lead you on,' she sobbed. 'How long are you going to keep punishing me for coming here to find out about Colette?'

She sat up and wiped her cheeks with shaking fingers, before getting to her feet. She stooped to pick

up her bikini top and put it on. Then a wild recklessness seemed to take hold of her and, humiliated
and boiling with rage, she began to walk back in the
direction of the house. She heard Marc call her
name but chose to ignore him. 'Come back,
Meredith!' He caught up with her before she had gone
very far.

'I won't!' She continued walking towards the house,
She was strangely disappointed when he made no
further effort to detain her.

In the afternoon the wind got up and the fronds
of the palms danced in the warm air. On returning
to her room, after lunch, Meredith discovered that
there was a straw basket, containing orchids, awaiting
her pleasure. She also made the discovery that somebody had collected the rest of her clothes from the
estate.

From the sliding doors to her balcony she could see
Marc doing a slow and powerful crawl across the
sparkling pool.

Her eyes were suddenly moody with rage. 'Jungle
creature,' she whispered. 'I detest you!'

All through dinner she refused to talk, unless it was
absolutely necessary.

'You are like a child in revolt,' he told her mockingly,
'but that is just fine with me. After all, revolt is healthy.
Now, stop this nonsense with me. You are both
beautiful and maddening, and you are beginning to
madden me, in no uncertain terms. It is a matter of
astonishment to me that I am so patient with you.
However, put it down to the fact that I have lost interest in you.'

A coldness spread around the region of her heart.
Nevertheless, she found herself saying, 'In that case,
let me go.'

'I will never let you go. With me marriage is for
ever. I also find that, with you, I have alternating feelings—the kind of feelings that go along with one's pos-

sessions. It pleases me to have a wife—even for decorative purposes only. I once mentioned to you, I think, that there have been women who have pampered me. Bear that in mind—you see, Meredith, I find that you are beginning to bore me.'

She received this crushing news without flinching. How, she did not quite know.

CHAPTER SEVEN

IN front of the small staff Marc was always pointedly attentive and so, outwardly, they appeared to be blissfully happy. They mostly ate out of doors, sitting on Indian straw chairs and screened by hibiscus, bougainvillea, oleander and waving palms. The sun gilded everything, including their already rich tans and Meredith's tawny blonde hair. There were no footprints other than their own on the strip of very private beach.

However, Marc made absolutely no move to touch her, and sometimes, as she lay stretched lazily at the poolside or on the beach, she wondered how she could hurt him. Instead, she spent long moments working on her finger and toenails, which were immaculately lacquered . . . and all the time she kept noticing all the trivial and endearing details about the man she had married. Sometimes, when she felt so stiff and tense that she was ready to break and shatter, she would slip into a silken or organdie caftan, for she had bought four from a Creole girl who had come to the house for this purpose, and walk along the magnificent island beach, stopping now and then to examine something that had been washed up by the sea.

At sunset, when the sky was a kingfisher-blue and streaked with orange, scarlet and pink, she would drink frothing daiquiris with Marc and eat Russian caviar until the sky was filled with stars. Often the people from the village came to play sega music for them.

Marc seemed to like showing her over the house and she would find herself relaxing with him.

'I've been admiring this carpet,' she said, on one such occasion, 'It's utterly beautiful.'

'Oh, that. . . .' He shrugged carelessly, but she was quick to notice that he was pleased. Looking down at the white rug which was patterned with huge pale blue elephants, he went on, 'It was probably made for the summer palace of a rajah . . . oh, maybe a hundred years ago. Who knows? *I* like to think so, anyway.'

On one occasion she infuriated him after he had shown her his collection of Oriental jades and porcelains.

'I enjoy collecting things,' he said. 'Collecting is a mature activity, after all.'

Before she could stop herself she said, 'Like collecting women, of course. Isn't that what you mean?'

'What would you like me to say?' His voice was coldly angry. 'That, searching for things that amuse me, I collect wives?'

'I didn't imagine that you went round collecting wives. You only have a wife now because you wanted to punish me and had nothing to lose. I know that, because you told me so yourself. I just meant women in general. You mentioned that—that women have pampered you.' She felt bitterness wash over her.

'Women can be, unfortunately—what is it they say? A pain in the neck. However, yes, for like art and if they happen to be beautiful, I like to possess them. If a woman is beautiful she demands attention, no? Like the possessions I have just shown you. Like a work of art, also, she likes to be seen, in very different circumstances and in different lighting. As in the case of sculptures, or artifacts, she is there to be fondled. Often on the other hand, though, this does not apply. Women, like art, demand attention, but more often than not, in the case of women, I do not wish to submit to their wiles. These days everybody seems to be living with giant trees in their houses. I prefer to live with things of beauty, like that carved Indian screen over there, for instance. That is—up to now. Now, I am saddled with a very difficult wife.'

'You know what to do,' she told him, her heart hammering.

'Yes, I do know what to do, and it is a view that even the most reluctant brides must regard with awe. . . .'

As she watched him walking away from her she wondered why she had spoilt everything—because she loved him so much, and anything was better than nothing.

The more inaccessible he seemed the more she yearned for him to touch her, but he remained baffling and confusing and kept her guessing. With savaged pride she began seriously to think of leaving somehow.

Sometimes, when he touched her, she felt the desire in her rise like a mountainous wave, whipped by a cyclone, while her troubled green eyes probed him.

In the desire she felt to have him notice her, she lost all sense of shame. She had amongst her clothes a daring and sensational bikini—so daring, in fact, that after purchasing it she had not dared to wear it. Now she decided to do so, and coming upon her at the poolside before lunch, Marc looked down at her. The sun slanted across her almost nude body and he went on staring at her for a moment before he said, 'You suggest everything, no? But reveal nothing. Why don't you take your bikini off and be done with it?'

She held her breath as he lowered himself beside her and then she watched his well-kept fingers, reach out to undo the ties of the tiny bra.

'Perhaps you are just aching to go topless?' She met his glance with her wide, green stare and his own dark eyes were hard as he watched her. 'God knows you are beautiful enough to go naked. Right now, you are at your most infuriating, do you know that?'

'Why?' she asked him. 'I'm merely working on my tan.' She clutched the tiny bra to her.

'What is this preoccupation with your tan?' he snapped. 'You are tanned enough. Seeing you like this, almost naked, infuriates me.'

To goad him she retorted, 'And, if you're honest, excites you.'

As usual Marc paled when his anger was aroused, and after a moment he said, 'What you want is to have your cake and eat it, no? Always a difficult request.'

'I don't have to listen to all this!' Her voice was taut and she made to stand up, but he was beside her in an instant and his fingers went to her wrist. There was only the hint of strength in them, but enough to make her subside.

'You *will* listen!' His voice had assumed an authoritative, arrogant tone. 'I do not like being made a fool of.'

'You told me that before,' she said. 'Why do you feel a fool at this particular moment, for goodness' sake? What have I done?'

'I did not say that I feel a fool. I said that I do not like being made a fool of. While you are swimming in this pool, or sitting or lying in the sun beside it, you will wear a reasonable swimsuit. Right? There is no need to tease me. I am not interested in your little tricks, which come and go like summer showers.' His eyes travelled down her tanned legs and Meredith knew a strange timeless sensation. Had he known anything when that faint shiver had passed through her, or had it been only on her side? Had he meant what he had said when he had told her that he had lost interest in her and that she bored him?

'You never fail to madden me,' he went on, then he stood up and looked down at her. 'I do not have to remind you, do I, that you are my wife and you will do as I say.' He spoke with the usual firm voice of one who is accustomed to giving orders and having them carried out.

Suddenly she felt very young and could not think of anything to say as she stared up at him. Then she began to fasten the tiny garment and knew a bleak moment of self-pity and contempt.

Marc went on regarding her. 'Do not start anything. You just may regret it.' His speech, now, was slow and deliberate. He might have been addressing a child.

'One would hope to find serenity on an island, Marc,' she said in a small voice. 'I'm afraid I haven't found it—not since stepping off that plane when I first arrived here.'

'Serenity is only to be found in distant Kyoto,' he replied, 'where a thousand years of meditating have shown the way to relaxation, peace and transcendence. Even the most beautiful residential neighbourhoods of Kyoto, the old capital of Japan, show the street only blank walls with perhaps an occasional gate, topped with tiles. Is this the kind of serenity to which you refer? I must endeavour to create this feeling for you— the feeling that you are in a Kyoto *tokonoma*. Or would you prefer a refectory on Mount Athosi in ancient Egypt? You name it, Meredith.'

'You're just trying to point out how ignorant I am, aren't you? Well, I'm not as ignorant as you choose to think . . . even though I thought fit to marry you!' She stood up in one easy movement and stalked off to her room, as she had grown to think of it.

There she idled through her bath and, later, lingered nude before one of the long mirrors. Feeling shamed and tense, she tried desperately to relax in a beautiful cane chair, wearing her black satin Chinese housecoat with the wisteria and blossoms embroidered upon it, and sipped the cool drink which she has poured for herself in glittering crystal. Shattered and depressed, she needed all the pampering there was at this moment. Placing the glass on the small cane glass-topped table at her side, she pulled her knees up to her chin, like a small girl, and wrapped her arms around her legs.

There was a knock on the door and she stared at the door for a moment, before going to open it. Maxula, one of the Creole maids, stood there. 'This is Katia,'

she said. 'She has come from the hotel beauty salon,
up the way, to give you a massage.'

Looking at the girls blankly, Meredith queried. 'A
massage?'

'Yes.' This time it was Katia who spoke. 'A scented
massage, using scented oils, rose and patchouli.'

'Patchouli? But I don't even know waht patchouli
is!' Meredith tried to laugh, to hide the embarrassment she was feeling.

'Patchouli is perfume got from an Indian plant,'
Katia replied.

'I honestly don't understand what this is all about,'
Meredith said. 'I—I didn't ask for this. There's been
some misunderstanding.'

'Monsieur de Chavagneux telephoned the hotel.
That is where I work—in the beauty salon.'

'Well,' Meredith stood back, 'this really baffles me—
but since you've come all this way, please do come in.'

At first she was stiff and embarrassed as the girl got
to work on her, and then she felt herself begin to relax,
giving herself up to the luxury of being massaged with
scented oils . . . a complete new experience, so far as
she was concerned.

'I'm amazed,' she said, when the massage was over.
'It was a marvellous experience, and I feel so relaxed.'

'So the women who patronise the beauty salon at
the hotel tell me,' Katia replied, smiling. 'I am glad
you have enjoyed it.'

Why had Marc gone to the trouble of arranging the
massage? Had he detected how tense and unhappy she
was? Was he sorry for her? Suddenly Meredith found
herself struggling with tears.

She did not go to lunch, however. Instead, she sent
word to Marc that she was not very well.

When he knocked and entered her room she was still
sitting in the cane chair, wearing her Chinese housecoat.

His eyes went over her. 'What is the matter with
you?'

'I'm not very hungry,' she told him.

'So? There must be a reason for this, surely?'

'Marc, I just don't want to eat lunch today. By the way, thank you for arranging the massage for me. I—it has a very relaxing effect.'

'In that case, you will enjoy your lunch.'

'I've told you—I don't want to eat. It's as simple as that.'

'It is not so simple. So now I am faced with a communications gap! Surprise upon surprise is one of the most tantalising elements in your make-up. Do you know that? You will eat lunch.' He spoke with scarcely controlled anger.

'Why is it so important for me to eat lunch? What's so important about lunch? I often skip lunch.' Her gold-brown face was unhappy.

She was aware of the vitality and impatience in him.

'I often find myself wondering about the speculation of my small staff here,' he told her.

'Well, I'm afraid I'm not interested in public speculation,' she replied, wishing that the floor would open up and swallow her.

'No, of that I am quite aware, and that is the trouble with you. You are not interested in a lot of things— like taking part in some sort of Mafia kidnapping. You were so uninterested in other people's feeling that you went about your plans coldly and calculatingly with this man Parker.'

'Can't we forget that?' She spoke quickly and on a hard breath. 'I've been made to suffer for my stupidity, haven't I?' I pay—every day of my life here. . . .' she broke off.

'You do not know what suffering is,' he cut in. 'Anyway, I will wait luncheon for you.'

Meredith felt a raging wildness come over her.

'I want to leave here,' she told him, getting to her feet. 'I can't go on here.'

'Don't worry,' Marc allowed a suitable time to

elapse, so that his words could sink into her, taking care to talk very slowly, 'you will be leaving here soon enough.'

Meredith felt her face go white. He *had* meant what he had said. He was bored with her. He no longer wanted her.

'Fine,' her voice sounded very faint. 'Well, that's just fine with me, actually.'

'I wish to discuss this with you during lunch,' he told her, before leaving the room.

After he had gone, she looked out thin cotton beach pyjamas—white with black—then she drew her sun-streaked blonde hair back from her face and her green eyes appeared enormous and very green in her tanned face.

She stood back and gazed at the unhappy face that belonged to her. 'Well,' she said very softly, 'I guess you could say your little Mafia show is coming to an end.' Suddenly she laughed. '*No?*' There was heart-break behind the word.

Her face was wooden when she joined Marc. He was decidedly irritable.

'I have gone out of my way to amuse you since we arrived here,' he told her, 'and today I had arranged a lunch which I hoped you would enjoy.'

Meredith made no reply but looked at the individual trays covered with old Chinese texts and arranged on a small linen-draped table which announced that the cuisine was going to be Oriental. Quail and dumplings were artistically arranged on plates and appointed with rice bowls and chopsticks. Green onions and parsley, characteristic ingredients, she knew by now, of Chinese cooking, provided sculptural table decoration. She noticed the dry white wine in an ice-bucket. The entire scene was reflected in the glittering pool. On a nearby table there was a dizzying profusion of fruits.

'I do not know why I bother,' Marc was saying.

'This is a play with only two actors, no?'

'Yes, I suppose it is,' she replied, then lowered her lashes.

'Well, it is nearly time for the curtain to come down,' he went on. 'We will be leaving this house in the near future.'

'I see.' She tried to keep the shock from her voice. 'Well, that—that's fine.'

Well, what has she expected? She had, after all, just as he had said, wanted to eat her cake and hang on to it at the same time.

'However, we will discuss this during our meal. Let me first mix you a very good drink,' he said.

At one corner of the pool area there was a profusion of batik-wrapped cushions in shades of peach, melon, ginger, turquoise and palm-green. Dusky-pink and coppery shaded bougainvillea swayed in the breeze. Meredith imagined there was the scent of sandalwood in the air.

Her unhappy eyes went to the sun-gilded beach, the palms and the turquoise sea. The house faced the sea and behind it, in the distance, were those strangely-shaped moutains.

Passing her a drink, Marc said, 'Soon you will be leaving, so let us drink to that.' He spoke on a note of mockery and she turned away from him.

'I'm waiting for you to be a little more specific,' she told him.

'That will have to wait. We will enjoy our drinks first.'

Meredith closed her eyes briefly as she tried to control her feelings.

The drink which he had poured for her tasted smoky, rich and sweet, and she was grateful for its obvious strength. The ice-cubes were cold as they touched her lips and her nerves were on edge.

'You go to a lot of trouble to—amuse me.' Her voice was bitter. 'There's really no need to amuse me. I don't know why you bother about me.'

'There are a lot of things you do not know.' Marc
seemed off hand and uninterested. She had the feeling
that he was taunting her and that this was becoming
all-absorbing. Suddenly, as if guessing her thoughts,
he lifted his thick dark lashes and caught her unawares
as she was in the act of giving him a moody stare.

'I often think,' he said, tearing a roll apart with those
well-manicured brown fingers, for they had now
started on their lunch, 'that it is a pity noblemen
abandoned fingers in favour of forks . . . that was about
four hundred years ago. It rather appeals to me, I
think, to use only fingers to eat an entire meal—and a
hunting knife, perhaps.'

'That's because you're nothing more than a modern-
day pirate,' Meredith replied hotly. He had stunned
her by hinting that their marriage, such as it had been,
was going to fall apart.

He laughed abruptly. 'So?' He went on eating, then
told her, 'You know, I had a silversmith hammer out
the figure of my brother's child's patron saint at the
end of a specially designed silver spoon. This spoon is
now the first of Colette's set of Apostle spoons. You
have heard of Apostle spoons?' When she made no
reply he said, 'You refer to me as a modern-day pirate.'
He glanced up at her with a kind of angry amusement.
'This is because I suggest that I would enjoy to use
the fingers while eating? In this house, you might have
noticed there is much china, crystal and silver,
customed-designed for my family. There is much more
in France, but it was acquired honestly. The family
crest has been sand-blasted or copper-wheeled
engraved, depending on the method of engraving.'

'There's no need to impress me, Marc. I think
you've gone out of your way more than enough to
amuse, impress and—hurt me. You mention that these
possessions were acquired honestly. . . .' Suddenly she
bit her lip and looked away. Then she lifted the

sparkling goblet to her lips and spilled a small quantity of wine. 'Your marriage to me was anything but honest.' She felt absolutely drained of emotion. 'However, I realise that it's coming to an end, because that's what you have to say to me, isn't it?'

'Adoring you as I do, I will never let you go. But no, Meredith, we are going to Paris.' There was a look of amusement in his dark, tawny-flecked eyes as he studied her, combined with an amused triumph in the tone of his voice.

She stared back at him with a disbelieving expression in her eyes.

'What for?' She spoke stiffly but felt strangely elated.

'We will travel with André and Colette, who is going to live there, with my sister Thierry and her husband Claude. In other words, the time is now ripe for this child to be taken to a place of safety—away from irresponsible people like you and this sugar magnate Parker and his nitwit daughter.'

A wave of remorse swept over her. Because she had agreed to come to Mauritius she had set a chain of events into motion. The position, now, was that Colette was going to be separated ever further from her mother and grandfather. In self-hating silence she sat there just staring at Marc.

'Oh no!' She shook her head in disbelief. 'No, Marc, don't do that!'

'What would you suggest, in that case? That the child remain here on the island, to be plagued by a man who professes to call himself her grandfather?'

'He *is* her grandfather, and you know it!' Numbly she stared at him. 'Besides, it's not fair to Colette. If she were to remain here in Mauritius, her mother would be able to visit her at least, and with so little trouble. It's a matter of principle.'

'Leave principles to me,' Marc snapped. 'I am more at home with them than you. The French nurse has no desire to leave the island. Therefore you will look after Colette on the flight.'

'I'm sorry, I can't agree to that.' Meredith rose to her feet and he was beside her in a flash and his fingers went to her wrist.

'Finish your lunch. Or I promise you, Meredith, I shall fly into a rage.'

Miserably, she said, 'All this has been my fault. . . .'

'I am not concerned at this stage with whose fault it is,' he told her.

Although she sat down again she made no attempt to eat and sat staring at the garden, seeing nothing.

For a while neither of them spoke and Marc continued with his meal.

'Getting across to you is like an obstacle course,' he said, breaking into her thoughts. 'My brother wished to marry this girl, but because she was under age at the time, her father refused his permission. No tassels, no cords—this is what the grandfather wishes. Anyway, why complain? You just wear yourself out. You are in this thing up to your neck, including your marriage to me. You waste your energy and mine. It is not what you expected, is it, to hear me talk about such plans?'

'You depress me,' she said, in a small voice.

'So? Why is that?'

'You're a cold and severe person.'

'Women always say that, when a man sees through them, he is cold and severe. Make no mistake, we are going to Paris.' He had been pouring wine and raised his eyes to her own.

Much to her despair Meredith began to cry very softly, then she got up and went to stand next to the white latticework.

'You are merely crying for yourself,' Marc's voice was hard. 'And what is more, you are crying for someone who is not worth it.'

'Thank you!' she swung round on him. 'You have

the power to hurt me. You seem to forget that I still happen to be your wife. I—I could—could *sue* you for treating me this way!'

'Ah, so now it is you who is reminding me?' There was no sympathy in this voice. 'Well, things are moving, no?'

'You're in a class of your very own,' she snapped, her temper rising and getting the better of her tears.

'Sure,' he shrugged carelessly. 'For sure. Anyway, you will, I think, enjoy Paris. My sister and her husband live in the de Chavagneux villa, near the Bois de Boulogne. It is a very interesting house. As a matter of fact, even at this early age Colette bears an extraordinary resemblance to my sister.'

'What you're trying to say is that Colette is a de Chavagneux through and through. I mean, the Parkers just don't exist, do they? Well, that's where you're so wrong, because they most certainly *do* exist, and have as much right to Colette as your brother does.' Her gaze locked momentarily with his. Her game of deceit had reached its full awesome potential, for she realised that, if she had refused to come to Mauritius, all this might never have happened.

Her eyes widened as Marc stood up and covered the short distance between them in a few strides and caught her to him and held her close, pinning her arms to her sides in a grip that hurt her.

'What is it with you?' His eyes were hard. 'I explained the position to you, did I not? That my brother wished to marry this flighty little girl.'

His eyes were remarkable, she found herself thinking, almost stupidly, of so dark a brown as to appear black at first sight, until you became aware of those tawny flecks, but as hard and fierce and glittering as a hawk's at this very moment.

His mouth moved to her throat and he kissed it with an almost brutal intensity, moving downwards to the hollow between her breasts.

'You know,' he said, finally, against her mouth, 'there are times when I could willingly thrash you.'

'You dare!' she exclaimed as he let her go.

Turning quickly, she ran in the direction of the house, where she locked herself in her room and wept as she had not wept before.

As she packed her personal possessions, she tried to shut her mind to everything else. She would not think of the past. She would concentrate only on the future, and the future was going to Paris, with Marc, because he still wanted her. The best she could do was to get word to Richard Parker and pray that all would turn out for the best.

Marc had explained that they would be going back to the estate before leaving Mauritius for France.

'If you wish to shop,' he had said, 'I would suggest that you do so in Paris. It is up to you, but I think you will enjoy this.'

With her thoughts busy on writing a letter to Richard Parker, and finding a suitable opportunity to post it, Meredith said, 'I do need one or two things quite urgently.'

'Well, that is fine. Soon after we get back to the estate I have to drive out to the laboratory and the Experimental Station. We will go there first and then continue to Curepipe.'

'You mean you'll be coming with me?' There was an edge to her voice.

'What is it this time? What are you planning now, Meredith?'

'Nothing. It just seems so ridiculous,' she explained, trying to halt the colour from surging into her cheeks. 'You enjoy keeping this carefully worked out little balance-sheet about me, don't you?'

'Can you blame me? I don't advise you to try and escape.' His voice was quiet and controlled.

She felt like sobbing out the whole truth to him— that she did not want to escape—that she loved him, but these things could not be said, only felt.

The evening before they left the beach house, they walked up the silky sands. The pounding of the surf on the reef reminded Meredith that she had believed her strange marriage to be over and was then reassured, almost immediately, that it was not. Relief flooded through her. Perhaps, she thought, this had been the jolt she had needed, for the next time Marc took her in his arms she would respond completely to his lovemaking.

It was all so beautiful—the palms leaning towards the water, the filao branches, at sunset, like a network of black lace, that stretch of incredible coastline. An old fisherman sat mending nets which were strung from tree to tree, forming a gauzy enclosure.

Impulsively Meredith said, 'I can't get over the beauty. All this—and that beautiful house. A beach house, as you call it, hardly describes it, Marc. Who drew the plans for you?' She turned her head to look at him and the wind blew her sun-streaked hair across her face and she shook it back.

'You do not really need plans for a house such as this.' She detected surprise in the tone of his voice. 'You don't have to work with T-squares. I did not bother with plans.'

'I find that hard to believe,' she said, and he laughed.

'You do? But no. I used my imagination and the imagination of my builder. We worked like—what shall I say?—a couple of sculptors. I made many sketches. He approved them. Sometimes he disapproved and we would start again. I spent hours walking about the site.' Marc stopped walking, suddenly, and turned to look back at the house in the distance, while Meredith stood next to him, aware of him and wanting him very desperately.

'I would try very hard to understand this piece of land, on which I wanted to build my house. I felt the sun. You know what I mean? I watched the direction of the winds and I came here, again at night, and I watched the stars. I gazed at the palms and I knew that the house must see those palms, too. So,' he shrugged, and laughed lightly again, 'I had windows put there, windows put here, sliding glass doors over there. To frame everything, you see. I was constantly in a very bad humour with everybody while I was busy thinking about this house.'

Without thinking, she replied, 'Yes, I can imagine that.'

Glancing at him again, she was acutely aware of the sensuality of his lips and another wave of longing came over her.

Suddenly she said impulsively, 'Marc, I had the feeling, often, that you were drawing me out. I should have confided . . . confessed. . . .'

He cut her short, and she knew that look. It could be intimidating. 'I am not concerned with that now. We have been over it all. For the moment, anyway, it is in the past. You know the position. Colette is going to live with my sister in Paris. When we get back from Paris we will start on making this marriage work. This time, you will play an active role. Up to now, I have shown you the patience of a saint.' He began to walk on, and for a moment she stood watching him.

When she had caught up to him he said, 'You are like mercury. Your name should have been Mercury, not Meredith. It is always a mistake to try and rake up the past. Don't you know that?'

'You've raked it up often enough,' she replied quickly. 'In fact you've never let me forget the past.' A bleak mood of self-pity took hold of her.

'I do not require a speech,' he said, 'especially now, at this stage, when I have sorted things out. You will also not refer to the past while we are in Paris. When we come back to Mauritius we will start again. I told you, I had nothing to lose when I married you. I lost the girl I loved, and yet I have everything to gain, no? Every man needs a mate, no?' He turned to look at her.

'And so you killed two birds with one stone.' Her voice was hard. 'You punished me, and at the same time you got yourself a—mate.'

'I realised, of course,' he went on, 'that the man who married you would have a hard time, because you are wanton—and disloyal. Nevertheless, without much effort I have achieved a very exciting and beautiful girl. What is more, a very eager girl, until she too discovered what it is like to be tricked, no? But we will change all that, when the time comes.'

'How can you call me wanton?' His remark seemed to take her by the throat and her green eyes were blazing with fury. 'I have never, and I repeat never, been wanton!'

'You are entitled to your opinion, of course.' His voice became almost taunting.

'You will never touch me again,' she added, and meant it.

'No?' He laughed shortly. 'Well, we will change that fast enough.'

Suddenly his hand went to her hair, tugging her head back so that her face was turned up towards his own. Then, drawing her to him with his free hand, he sought her lips hungrily, with a violence that frightened her.

Her hands went to his shoulders and her fingernails bit into him as her body began to consume itself in flame, firing his even more. She lost all sense of shame in the thrill of having him close to her again. This time, she thought wildly, there would be no turning back. All she knew was that she wanted him, under any conditions.

When he released his hold on her he said, 'I am, after all, in a careful mood, I find.'

Meredith stood staring at him with shocked eyes. 'Come,' he said, taking her hand. 'I brought you here to watch the glorious colours of the sunset. They are enough to add romance and magic to any situation— but nevertheless, I find that I am in a careful mood. For you see, with you, I never know what is going on inside that head of yours.'

'What do you expect me to do?' she asked brokenly. 'Have hysterics because you—you—I allowed you to arouse me, and then you calmly rejected me?'

'I have discovered something for myself.' He took her face in his hands and kissed her forehead, and when he straightened, his half-smile was a little crooked, affectionate almost. 'And that is, you are very uncontrolled. The point is, I knew this, but I still wished, for various reasons, to make you my wife. I still wish it, even if it does take patience to put up with you.'

'Let me go,' she begged. 'I want to leave this island. Release me, Marc . . . let me go!' It was like a cry.

'Why should I submit to such a thing? I told you, I have reached the stage when I need a wife . . . a mate . . . a mother for my children. I am the only sugar planter, I think, in the whole of Mauritius who has not taken a wife.' His dark eyes held a gleam of mockery. 'You are beautiful. You are maddening, but you will do me very well.'

'I'm tired of fighting you,' she said, in a small voice.

'So? Well . . .' he lifted his shoulders, 'I am glad you realise that you have lost.'

'This whole thing is a—a mess!' she sighed.

She watched him as he reached for a strand of her windswept hair. 'Your hair is a—mess,' he said, 'at the moment. But it is still very beautiful.'

They left the house the following morning and drove straight to the estate. Turning to her in the car, Marc said, 'It follows that I have a busy time ahead of me, before leaving for Paris. You will have to amuse yourself.'

'What about my job at the laboratory?' she asked.

'You will forget about your job at the laboratory.'

There was impatience in his voice.

With the best grace she could manage she asked, 'Has somebody else taken my place?'

'The position was held by André until he thought it wise to move to another part of the island—for obvious reasons. We managed to get along before you arrived, Meredith. I am sure you cannot see how—but we did manage. André will take up his post in the laboratory when we get back from Paris—or soon afterwards.'

'This island isn't very large,' Meredith ventured to say. She spoke in an angry and defiant voice. 'I daresay Richard Parker would have found out his whereabouts, and Colette's in time—without my help.'

'Well, yes, no doubt. But he engaged you to do this for him, no? Anyway, enough is enough. Do me a favour, Meredith please. Keep quiet.'

'You mentioned that you—that *we* would be going to the laboratory and Experimental Station and then on to Curepipe. Is this correct?' She was thinking of the letter which she intended to write to Richard Parker and she was trying to fathom out how she could post it without Marc's knowledge.

He turned and gave her a mocking smile. 'Yes. It will be another case of killing two birds with one stone.'

Three! she thought. Because she would have no option but to ask somebody at the laboratory to apply the necessary postage stamp and post her letter.

It was a glorious day and the twisting road was quiet. Meredith's eyes rested on the undulating canefields. There were glimpses of that breathtaking sea with the white surf breaking on to the coral reef and the beaches which were so like creamy meal, even from a distance. Red, pink and yellow poinsettia on the side of the road waved in the breeze. She had come to accept the carts drawn by hump-backed bullocks—so much a part of the island, with its palms and oleander bushes, just as she had got used to seeing a public wash-place where perhaps, as was the case at this very moment, a beautiful Creole girl would be splashing her deliciously long, bronzed legs and arms, using a great tablet of shocking-pink soap.

Beside her, Marc was wearing white linen pants and a pale gold silk shirt which was open to the waist. He was tanned and incredibly handsome, without a gram of extra weight on him.

In a gambling mood of recklessness she said, 'You've never told me that you love me, even when you were—you know—being swept along on a tide of—passion.'

He seemed suddenly to have frozen himself into an impersonal remoteness, and then he said, very softly, 'You have to be very sure, before you say, I love you. No?'

'That's sheer cynicism.' Her voice was hot.

'I prefer to call it irony,' he replied easily. 'Have you ever told *me* that you love me?'

The sight of the poetical charm of the stately Colonial mansion brought a - lump to Meredith's throat.

She had been to a dream house above a dream strip of beach, and she was still a wife in name only.

CHAPTER EIGHT

PARIS greeted them with its boulevards, planted with plane and chestnut trees and birds flying over the boulevards, fountains, pavement cafés, beautiful clothes in beautiful shops, many exciting eating-places, cake shops—*patisseries*—perfume shops, *coiffeurs*, intricate wrought-iron balconies, European jean-clad jet-setters and sweepers at work.

As she absorbed it all from the car, Meredith almost forgot the reason for her visit to one of the world's greatest cities.

Before leaving Mauritius, there had been shopping to do for little Colette de Chavagneux and for herself and when André had not been present, Marc *had*—and it had been impossible to get word to Richard Parker at that stage. Something would have to be sorted out in Paris, she told herself.

Thierry Jourdan, Marc's sister, met the plane and when she had been introduced to Meredith she exclaimed, 'Oh, but you are so *beautiful*!' She drew the word out on a long breath. Swinging round, she went on, 'But, Marc, why did you not tell me how beautiful this girl was?'

'For the very simple reason that you did not ask me.' There was a devilish, carefree look about him.

Before leaving the airport, Meredith had stood a little to one side, watching with moody green eyes the meeting up of the family. Tall, slim and pale, with fascinating almond-shaped green eyes, Thierry looked sad as she met Colette for the first time. Colette, on the other hand, was too young to understand what it was that was happening to her.

Eventually Thierry said, 'Claude was unable to come

along. He is very busy at the moment at his office, but
in any case,' she laughed charmingly, 'there would have
been no room for Claude in the car. Come along, my
darlings.' Her voice was assured, husky and low.

Thierry drove fast and efficiently, and from her seat
in the back of the long, sleek car, Meredith gazed and
gazed at Paris.

Breaking into her thoughts, Thierry asked, 'This is
your first visit to Paris, Meredith?' The strange
almond-shaped eyes met those of Meredith's in the
rear-view mirror.

'Yes, and as you can imagine, I'm very excited,'
Meredith answered. She felt nervous and unsure of
herself.

'Paris is a little dirty, maybe,' Thierry shrugged elegant shoulders, 'but romantic, for sure. It is also a little
irritable, for you see,' she laughed lightly, 'nobody goes
to bed. I think you will like it, though . . . the romantic
river, the bird-sellers, the booksellers, the bridges. The
river cuts Paris in half, you know. Our boulevards are
the best in the world. Don't you agree, Marc?'

'Definitely . . . pathways within the city. But then
everything is better in Paris. In any case, you do not
have to sell Paris to Meredith, Thierry. I think she is
hooked already, no?' He took Meredith's hand in his
own. 'What do you say, my darling?'

She had the feeling that he was putting on a show
for his sister's sake.

'Yes, it's beautiful,' she replied.

'And everywhere the touring coaches,' Thierry went
on lightly, turning into a narrow cobbled street and
then leaving it behind again. 'By the way, Meredith,
one must be careful of pickpockets in Paris.'

Meredith made an attempt to join in the conversation. 'I keep noticing the stone walls and stonework.
Everything appears so ancient, and yet so elegant. I
love the lamps too, like clusters of balloons on those
massive ironwork bases—or pedestals. . . .' She

laughed and then bit her lip, feeling young and ignorant among these people. 'I can't think what you call them,' she ended a little helplessly, and wishing that she could be left to herself so that she could try to count down.

'Marc will have told you, no doubt, that our house is in Neuilly, which is separated from Paris only by the Bois de Boulogne, but the air seems quite different.' She shrugged again and laughed that carefree laugh. 'Or so we like to think, anyway. Oh, to be sure, it is not exactly in the country, but it feels as if it is. I think you will like the house. It is very classic, very quiet, very Parisian. It is, I always think, a beautifully proportioned house and it contains mostly Louis Seize pieces, collected by our grandfather—the one who went to Mauritius—our father and some from Claude's family. The streets are lined with high walls, and beyond those walls, Meredith, comes the most exotic fragrances of the most beautiful gardens. There are swimming-pools—some people like to have a tennis court. We do not have a tennis court. In our house, our father used to give the most magnificent parties in Paris. Do you remember Marc? André?'

'He was well known for his lavish hospitality,' André replied, but his thoughts seemed far away.

Marc, on the other hand, appeared relaxed and at ease as he went on caressing Meredith's slender, tanned wrist with his fingers. To all outward appearances they must appear the most ardent lovers, she thought bitterly.

Suddenly Thierry started to giggle. 'And do you remember that time when Grandfather came from Mauritius on a vacation? The time when he insisted on having shrubs, plants and trees, which flourish in Mauritius, planted in the garden? He had the idea that the soil was as lush and as fertile as that of the island.'

'Many of them *did* grow,' said Marc, also laughing, 'did they not?'

'Yes,' Thierry shook her head and wiped a tear of laughter from the corner of one eye. 'Oh, my, *Grandfather!*' There was an awkward silence and then Thierry rushed on, 'And here you are. And Marc—so much in love!'

'As you say, so much in love.' Marc's voice was caressing, almost, as he lifted Meredith's fingers to his lips. When she turned her head to look at him his dark eyes met hers with a hint of amusement in them, while a faint smile tugged at his mouth.

'I think you will be happy here,' Thierry went on. She seemed eager to talk—for there to be no silences. 'Our house stands on one of the most unchanged streets in Neuilly. It is well hidden and completely at peace. It is a family mansion, and yet these two brothers of mine decided to leave it when Marc inherited the sugar plantation, bequeathed to him by my grandfather who went there so many years ago, and died there. By the way, I have prepared the most romantic guest-room in the house for you—for the honeymooners.' Although she was talking, almost without ceasing, Thierry gave careful attention to the traffic. 'As a matter of fact, the room was redecorated. I must have had a premonition. I had a new canopy of Scalamandré silk taffeta made for the bed.'

At this piece of information, Meredith's heart turned right over, it seemed. Beside her she could feel the weight of Marc's amused look on her face and her body.

The de Chavagneux residence, now occupied only by Claude and Thierry Jourdan, and a small staff, was in fact nothing like the usual private Parisian house, with a small courtyard and garden. It was surrounded by tall trees and sweeping lawns and, to Meredith's mind, was reminiscent of a foreign embassy and she could imagine vast sweeps of staircases with galleries, oil-paintings of ancestors, handsome bronzes and highly polished tables.

Parking the car, Thierry told her, 'In the springtime, after dinner, it is an enchanting experience to stroll out into the garden. None of the noises of Paris, you see, and Paris not even five minutes away.'

'But Paris, nevertheless, a backdrop for the home of my very charming sister. Paris has the compelling excitement which provides a perfect setting for Thierry, as I am sure, Meredith, you have already noticed.' Marc spoke good naturedly and affectionately.

When they were at last alone in the guest suite with its beautiful and fanciful treatment of blossom-strewn silk taffeta, in shades of pink, copper, amber and tender leaf-green, and painted and gilded medallion bed headboard, Meredith said, 'It's not possible for me to sleep in this bed with you, Marc, and you know it.'

Easily he said, 'You must *make* it possible.'

'What does your sister think she is doing to me?' She felt unreasonably angry towards the beautiful Thierry.

'My sister does not know of your deceit,' he told her, and his tawny-flecked eyes were suddenly cold and unforgiving.

Meredith's eyes went to the ornate bed, fit for a princess and which stood on a huge, heavily fringed off-white rug, which had obviously been handloomed in Mexico and which contributed to the mood of luxurious softness. Then she made a quick survey of the room, as if looking for a way out of having to share the huge bed with Marc.

One wide white windowsill was filled with a cluster of flowering plants in ornamental pots. They were there to welcome the lovers.

Marc closed the distance between them. 'Meredith,' he said, 'you will put up a show for my sister and for her husband Claude. André, of course, is another matter. He knows everything.'

'And yet he seems to like me,' she felt the need to say. 'At least *he* doesn't go out of his way to humiliate me and constantly remind me of the reason for my visit to Paris.'

Marc was wearing a pale beige Yves Saint Laurent lightweight suit, and she watched him as he wrenched off his tie and tossed it on to the bed. With an odd little thrill she watched him undo all the buttons of his shirt. The desire to touch his suntanned body was almost overpowering. He raised dark eyes.

'You—you don't know how you hurt me, sometimes,' she stammered.

'Sometimes I *mean* to hurt you.' His eyes were on her face. 'However, while we are here in Paris, we will make the best of things. We will be the perfect lovers, in other words. I want to be happy with Thierry and Claude and, as far as possible, with you. Do you understand this?'

'No,' she whispered, 'I'm afraid I don't understand this. I have no experience of being married to a man who despises me—and what's more,' she jerked her head in the direction of the beautiful bed, 'of having to sleep in a huge bed with him.' She shook her hair back from flushed cheeks and went on, 'How am I supposed to act? Tell me that!'

'You are supposed to act as though we are in love. It is as simple as that.' Marc pulled his shirt off and then went to one of their cases, which had already been sent up to the room. 'Do you wish to change?' he asked. 'Shall I open your case for you?'

'I hope I'll be able to laugh about this one day.' Her voice was bitter and unhappy. 'Laugh in the same carefree way as you're able to laugh about your grandfather's wish to grow island plants in Paris.'

He swung round. 'Laugh *now*. What more do you want? We have accomplished our mission. Colette is safe in the de Chavagneux residence, where she will be well cared for. She will remain here until André chooses to marry some woman and takes her back, wherever that might be—I don't know. And so we take in Paris . . . by night and by day. Grab—is that what they say, in certain circles—what you can and when you can.'

'I notice the word grab, of course. You always think of me as a grabber, don't you?' Meredith experienced a huge feeling of disappointment and frustration, but she had asked for it. She knew that.

Ignoring her remark, Marc said, 'There is one other thing.'

'And what is that?' she asked.

'You are wholly and unquestionably woman and you are my wife, and I want to enjoy what is unquestionably mine. We are going to have a love-affair in Paris, in other words.' There was a wealth of meaning to his words and she felt her heart accelerate.

'I am also killing two birds with one stone,' he went on. 'For you see, I came also specifically to attend an annual meeting with the family lawyer. It suited very well, actually—this visit.'

Before lunch, he showed her over the house.

Double doors led into the salon, where the walls were hung with silk, and although she was certainly no connoisseur, Meredith was quick to notice the perfection of décor. In a recent portrait, an artist had captured the aristocratic beauty of Thierry.

In yet another room there was an extensive collection of sculpture, and she experienced an acute feeling of international ignorance.

'Thierry and Claude have added to the fine collections of art and antiques we have inherited—that is Thierry, André and myself,' Marc explained. 'Her primary interest is in décor, you might say. That and collecting.'

'You mean that some of the—things—you're showing me belong to you, then?' she asked. 'I'm being curious, by the way. I'm not interested in your possessions.'

'Yes. But here it will remain in this house. That is

right and fitting, I believe. André is of the same opinion—although there are some items which we have already established in Mauritius.'

'It's all very interesting,' she admitted, 'And I feel so—inadequate. . . .'

'You need not feel that way.'

'Well, I do. And—the house?' she ventured to ask.

'This house remains in the family. It is a very tied-up, complicated situation—and there are other properties. This explains the annual meetings with the family lawyer.'

'Will you ever come back, do you think?'

'That presents a teasing question. But no, I think not. You see, I am quite happy with my sugar plantation and my beach home. I am still not quite sure why *I* inherited the estate. André was already trained as a chemist, and so, with certain changes, it all fitted in.'

'It's an unusual name—Thierry,' she commented.

'It was my mother's maiden name,' he told her.

'So it's a surname?' She was surprised.

'Yes.'

'But it's beautiful! So is your sister, by the way. She's absolutely stunning.'

'So are you.' Marc took her into his arms and he kissed her lingeringly, his lips moving to the low cut of her dress, and she experienced a dawning apprehension as to what she was going to be like with him in the king-size bed beneath the blossom-strewn silk taffeta canopy. This time, she knew very well, she was prepared to swallow her pride and allow him to make love to her and, what was more, she would go to him with complete, and sweet, she hoped, abandon.

His lips were warm and firm and his kisses slow-moving, depriving her of all power of thought. One arm went upwards and his fingers were on her neck, moving upwards slowly until they were in her tawny-blonde hair. He kept on kissing her, and all the time his fingers caressed the shape of her head, beneath all that glorious hair. On the taut skin over her skull the movement was possessive, somehow—more possessive than if he had cupped her bare breast, and the sensation was nothing short of some wonder drug causing her to float away in a mist. She could feel the warmth of him, as she sagged against his body, becoming so much a part of him that his heartbeat was as though it belonged to her.

'I will never let you go,' he whispered, against her mouth. 'I find you—far—too—exciting, far too desirable.'

Desirable, she thought. Desirable. No mention of love. Would he ever grow to love her? Somehow she thought not, and a feeling of utter despair rocked her.

Marc held her back from him and looked into her eyes, and then kissed her again.

'I hope I did not interrupt anything?' It was Thierry's husky voice. 'My darlings, there is just time for a drink before luncheon. I am sure you must feel like a drink, no? I did not even ask after your flight. What was it like?'

'A—a little bumpy at times, maybe.' Marc shrugged. 'High, buffeting winds—you know the sort of thing that goes on up there. Meredith was often very nervous. Weren't you, my darling?'

Trying to hide the strain of her smile, Meredith said, 'I don't really like flying, I'm afraid.'

'And Colette? She was not difficult?' Thierry wanted to know.

'No, she really was very good,' Meredith replied. 'Marc has been showing me everything. It's all so very beautiful.'

'I am glad you like it. Those chairs, by the way, are Louis Seize and signed by Séné—but there I go again!' Thierry laughed lightly.

Drinks were served in a less formal living-room, overlooking the garden and a pool reflecting wisteria.

Meredith glanced about the lovely room as she

accepted a glittering crystal glass from Marc. There were masses of flowers everywhere. She was growing used to luxury, she found herself thinking, amazed and a little excited. It was strange to think that she was part of it—part of the de Chavagneux family.

Bright-hued walls the colour of the inside of a ripe watermelon highlighted an immense white fireplace, which stretched up to the heavily-beamed ceiling and there were two seating arrangements in the room, one near the fireplace and one at the other end of the room. Pillow-laden sofas flanked large, glass-topped round tables and glittering chandeliers hung over each area. Roses and other flowers were arranged everywhere and the room was fragrant with them.

'This is my favourite room,' said Thierry. 'Little Colette has had her lunch and she is now taking a nap. So? How am I doing?' She glanced at André. 'You see, I will look after this small girl of yours very well.'

'I know you will.' André sounded tense, as usual.

'I still cannot understand why this girl will not marry you,' Thierry went on. 'It does not make sense.'

'The reason is simple. She is not of age and her father will not give his permission.' The tone of André's voice indicated that he no longer wished to discuss the subject.

'But you *wish* to marry her?' Thierry's almond-shaped green eyes were troubled.

'Of course!' André's voice was abrupt. 'What do you think? Of course I wish to marry the mother of my child. I happen to love her. But that is no reason why my child should stay with her grandfather, which is what *he* wants. No, no.' Suddenly he broke off and glanced in Meredith's direction. 'I am sorry,' he said, and Meredith was well aware of Thierry's enquiring eyes swinging round to her direction.

Double white doors led into the beautiful dining-room with its pastel silk wall-covering and matching drapes.

'You will notice,' Thierry addressed her brothers, 'that at long last I have got my chairs for this room.' She seemed intent in making light conversation. 'My primary interest in life is in décor and decorating, Meredith, so forgive me if I become a bore, will you? You see, I have made a point of adding to our father's collection of art and antiques. These, by the way, are authentic Renaissance curule chairs.'

'I'm afraid I'm not clued up about such matters,' Meredith replied. 'I'm none the wiser—but they are magnificent. They make me think of Roman chairs, beautifully covered and fringed to your wishes and to match this room.' She felt so ignorant in the presence of this distinguished French family, and the realisation that she had married into it was nothing short of staggering. 'What does curule mean? I'm ashamed to admit that I don't know.' She bit her lip and looked at Marc, then dropped her lashes as she picked up her melon-pink table-napkin.

'There is nothing to be ashamed of, my darling.' His voice was softly caressing as he began to lead her on the way to that moment when they would share the huge, canopied bed upstairs. 'But in any case, it means, I think . . . belonging, pertaining to any high dignity. Am I right?' He turned, laughing a little, to Thierry, who applauded him by lightly clapping her hands.

During the meal Meredith glanced about the room, taking in the superb eighteenth-century Aubusson tapestry, the round table at one end of the room, which displayed snuff-boxes, with miniature portraits on the lids . . . Louis Seize, no doubt. She fought back a little smile, but felt quite overwhelmed, never the less.

After lunch Marc took her out in a small, exciting car which belonged to Thierry, and Meredith took this time off to wonder about the girl he had been engaged to and who had lost her life in a skiing accident in the Alps. Had they driven round Paris, exchanging tender looks and holding hands? Had they slept together in a secret apartment on the Marais, somewhere—that charming old section of the city, centred around the Place des Vosges and overlooking the bridges along the Seine, which he had just shown her? Had they visited Montmartre, the Place du Tertre, place of rebellious artists and bohemian life-style, and had they been tempted to buy a painting for the apartment? Suddenly she felt like crying.

Startling her out of these thoughts, he said, 'What are you thinking about?'

'Just looking at everything,' she answered. 'I have never seen so many beautiful girls, so beautifully turned out. I feel absolutely dowdy by comparison. It's very obvious to me—or *even* to me, I should say, because I really know so little—that Thierry is dressed by Pierre Cardin.'

Because of the density of the traffic he did not look at her, but took her hand in his own. 'You wear clothes that are not only chic, but you always add that very individual touch . . . like the butterflies, no? But no, Meredith, you were thinking of something else. What was it?'

'I wasn't thinking of *something*,' she said, after a moment. 'I was thinking of a girl.'

'So? What girl?'

'The girl you were in love with—if you must know.' Her voice was very soft and Marc had to ask her to repeat what she had said.

'Why think of these things?' His voice was angry now. 'What is more important—why talk about them?'

'You asked me what I was thinking about,' she replied, stung. She took her hand away and stared out of the window.

They were on the avenue Kléber now, and the traffic seemed to surge in all directions. Cars came in every colour beneath the sun and many were driven, quite effortlessly, by smart, clued-up-looking girls. It was easy to see that they were in the world's most sophisticated capital, thought Meredith, a little dazed.

'Have you not yet learned the value of silence where some things are concerned, Meredith?' Marc asked, going back to where they had left off ten minutes ago.

She made no reply but sat there, cold and resentful, not looking at him.

'Tonight we will go to the Moulin Rouge.' His voice was suddenly gentle. 'You would like that? If you are not too tired? I have already booked, as a matter of fact, but these things can be changed. We are not going to be here for so long, so we must make the best of it, don't you agree?'

'I'd like that,' she said, 'very much. Who will be going?'

'Just the two of us. I mentioned to you that we would be having a love affair in Paris—and *with* Paris.'

In an endeavour to enter into the spirit of things she said, 'It sounds exciting. Have you noticed, Marc, that there are dogs everywhere—almost like Mauritius, except that these dogs are mostly poodles and very dainty on their leashes. There are dogs asleep in doorways and on pavements. The only difference is that they're not dying on their feet, like on the island.'

'I have already explained to you why they die on their feet in Mauritius. It is something we cannot understand, I know. Dogs are not "put to sleep" in Mauritius, even when they are old and unwanted, sometimes.' There was a rasp of impatience in his voice again. 'Look, what is it with you? Why are you so troubled?' He turned the car towards a steeply cobbled, and very narrow, hill and when he had parked it so that they could enjoy a breathtaking view of the city he turned to look at her.

It was true, she thought, looking at him. She was troubled and unhappy, when she could have been so happy. She had already made up her mind, even while talking about the unhappy and unfortunate starving dogs of Mauritius, who were left, because of religious beliefs, to die a natural—and so often such an unnatural death—to write to Richard Parker when they got back to Thierry's house. How she was going to post this letter was another matter. If only something could be sorted out for André and the girl he loved!

'Forget the past,' Marc was saying, and she returned his gaze. 'Do us both a favour, at least while we are in Paris, and forget it. It is too bad that your sugar magnate was outsmarted and you along with him, but he *has* been outsmarted and, so far as I am concerned, that is that. The present now belongs to us. Right?' He smiled, a little crookedly.

'Okay,' she said. 'I'm sorry.'

'Don't be sorry,' he said.

It was becoming cloudy. 'I hope it does not rain,' said Marc. 'Time, as you can imagine, has not permitted sightseeing this afternoon, for there is much to see, as you know. It will take days . . . but I wanted you to get the *feel* of Paris by just driving around at random. We will go back now. Tomorrow I am going with Thierry and André to our family lawyer.'

Thinking about the letter she wanted to write and post to Richard Parker, she said quickly, 'What will *I* do?'

'Claude will be there to keep you company, because he will be leaving his office after lunch tomorrow.'

Meredith felt dismayed. 'But I don't even know him!'

'You will get to know him this evening, before we leave for the Moulin Rouge. Don't worry, you will like Claude. Everybody likes him.' He placed his fingers beneath her chin and then kissed her, very lightly, on the lips. 'And so you like my sister?'

'Yes, very much.'

'I nearly forgot—I have a small gift for you.'

Meredith watched him as he felt in his pocket for a satin-quilted jewel-case.

'Why am I to receive a gift?' She was smiling now, in a better mood.

'Is not a surprise better than a reason?' His voice was teasing, as he watched her opening the case.

She caught her breath. Looking down at the string of glowing pink pearls, she said softly, 'Oh, I'm terribly thrilled, Marc! Thank you.'

Because she was so mixed up, so happy, and yet so desperately unhappy, she felt like crying. She had lost weight, she knew, but the new hollows in her cheeks only served to make her more starkly beautiful, as did the hollows in her shoulders and throat.

'I am glad you like them.' Already Marc was starting the car. 'The weather has decided to be unkind to us, but I do not think it will last.'

Claude Jourdan was distinguished in an impeccably tailored suit and he had romantic prematurely silver hair. His skin was naturally dark and tanned to an even deeper bronze. A pair of darkish green eyes, of hypnotic intensity, almost, bored into Meredith's, and she liked him immediately. However, in spite of herself, she was nervous. These were such sophisticated people, she thought, but apart from that, she constantly had the feeling that she was dying from shame and humiliation from the part she had played in having Colette brought to France.

'I am so pleased you and Marc could come,' Claude was saying, making matters worse for her.

'Thank you. I'm loving it.' Meredith bit her lip and then took a sip of her drink.

They were in the room in which they had enjoyed cocktails before lunch. She and Marc still had to bath and change for the Moulin Rouge.

'I am very cross with the weather,' Thierry said. A drizzling rain was falling monotonously now, occasionally coming down in a solid downpour. 'Parking can be so difficult, but I am sure Marc will do his best. I am thinking about the Moulin Rouge, of course.'

'I'll take an umbrella,' said Meredith, then felt her

cheeks flush. It sounded perfectly ridiculous—for who but a country bumpkin would take an umbrella to the Moulin Rouge? She could have bitten her tongue.

However, Thierry said, 'It would be a wise move.'

'I have met Colette,' Claude was saying, 'and just before you arrived, I was telling André how captivated I am by this small girl. She is very good and has completely taken to her new nurse. And so you are not dining with us?' He gave his attention to Meredith again.

'We have to fit in as much as possible while we're here,' she said shyly.

'Of course. It will be like another honeymoon for you—not that I should imagine the first honeymoon is over. But of course you must make the best of it while you are in Paris, I quite agree.'

Finally it was time to go upstairs and prepare for the Moulin Rouge.

'I see that, apart from the bathroom, there's a dressing-room,' Meredith ventured to say.

'Yes, there is, but I am not prepared to sleep in it, if that is what you mean,' Marc replied, and she recognised the desire he felt for her, the undeniable hunger in those strange dark eyes with the tawny flecks.

Staring back at him, she wanted him; ached for him.

'May I take a bath first?' she asked.

'Of course.'

Then she began walking about the lovely room, senselessly opening and closing cupboard doors and drawers, and she knew that he was watching her with considerable amusement.

'Look,' he said, after a few moments, 'why don't you go and bath?'

'I was looking for something,' she replied, not looking at him. 'M-my hair looks a mess.'

He came over to where she was standing and touched the nape of her neck with his lips. 'Your skin is so smooth and silkily tanned, and your hair does not look a mess.'

'My tan is beginning to fade, I think.' It was not easy to speak calmly. 'Okay, then,' she expelled a little breath and glanced about. 'I—I think I've got everything. . . .'

Moving away from him, she crossed to the marble-lined bathroom and closed the door, leaning against it with her eyes closed. To lock or not to lock? It was all so ridiculous, she thought, and left it unlocked as she filled the bath with water.

She was towelling herself dry when Marc knocked on the door, and before she could think what to say or do, he had opened it, and her green eyes were wide as she gazed at him from over the towel which she was clutching beneath her chin.

'Do not look so startled,' he said.

'I am startled.' Water still clung to her face in tiny silver drops.

'Oh? Why?'

'It's—embarrassing, that's why!'

'Embarrassing? Where is the embarrassment?' His smile was one of genuine amusement. 'Have you forgotten that you are my wife and that I have seen you topless?'

'This is the first time we've shared a bathroom—the first time we have shared a bedroom, for that matter. Marc, why did you come in here?'

'Are you not woman enough to know? This affair has progressed beyond the limit of sanity.' His eyes went over her. She looked touchingly young. 'Did you enjoy your bath?'

'Yes.'

'Why do you hold the towel so desperately? I have not reached this age without having seen the body of a woman before.' His tension communicated itself to her, however.

If the remark was intended to hurt her, it succeeded

in doing so. 'I'm sure you have,' she answered, in a choked little voice. Angry and hurt, she purposely allowed the towel to fall away from her, revealing her nakedness, and was quick to notice the change of expression in his eyes. Then she draped it about her and left the bathroom.

Perhaps she should start to tease *him*, she thought fiercely, as she began to dress. Walking about the room, she began to feel an anger building up inside her, a feeling of self-hatred, and she began to wonder what conceivable reason there could be for the existence of her marriage to Marc de Chavagneux.

While he was in the bathroom she scribbled a letter to Richard Parker, suggesting that he should come immediately to Paris, with his daughter, in an effort to patch up a tragic affair, explaining that André was desperately in love with the mother of his child and wanted to marry her. Then she sealed the envelope and dropped the letter into the small bag which she intended taking along with her to the Moulin Rouge.

The darkness was filled with wonder, for although a fine rain blurred the outline of Paris, there was an unexpected beauty about the city as lights sparkled and trembled in a confusion of reds, greens, gold, and orange.

'Do you know,' said Marc, 'in the thirties large areas of Paris were still lit by gas? There are some interesting stories about Paris.'

'Actually, I'm not disappointed that it's raining,' she said. 'The lights are beautiful in the glittering streets.'

'You are looking very sleek and fashionable,' he told her.

'Thank you,' she answered. 'Except for the little purple umbrella, but we're going to need it. You can see for yourself.'

'Of course.'

She was wondering how on earth she could post the letter to Richard Parker. If only she had a stamp! As it was, she was going to have to ask somebody to accept the necessary amount for the stamp and to trust that somebody to post the letter for her.

Marc managed to get parking space within a short distance to the entrance of the night-club and then they ran, laughing in the rain and sheltering, to the best of their ability, beneath the umbrella, towards the glass doors, leaving behind the lights and noises of the city.

'That was not so bad, was it?' he said, while Meredith shook the rain from the umbrella and then rolled it very carefully. They were not wearing coats, and as they prepared to enter the club one of the girls at the counter called out, 'Your umbrella, please.'

Thinking of the confusion, afterwards, of having to collect it, Meredith said, 'I'm going to take it with me.'

'It is not permitted. I am sorry.'

Feeling a fool, Meredith crossed over to the counter. It was at this moment that she thought about the letter.

Taking it from her bag, she asked the girl, who was attending to her ticket for the umbrella, if she could possibly post the letter for her, and the girl, sensing the urgency behind the request, agreed to arrange for a stamp, certainly, and the posting of the letter.

'Thank you,' Meredith said quietly. 'You just don't know how grateful I am.'

'It is a pleasure.'

When they were seated at a white-clothed table for two Meredith exclaimed, 'But, Marc, it's so *huge*!'

He laughed his gay and infectious laugh and she was saddened that, because of their tumultuous marital status, he did not laugh often enough.

'So?' He took her hand. 'You are glad we came? Even though you are most probably very tired.'

'I'm not tired—or if I was, I'm not now.'

'Good, because before the floor show we will dance,' he said. Amidst the murmur of conversation, the subdued laughter and clinking of glasses and cutlery, they were quite alone.

He held her close while they danced. 'You look so serious,' he said. 'What is it this time?'

Meredith tilted her head back and laughed softly. 'You probably won't believe me, but I was wondering where the floor show takes place, actually. I believe it's absolutely spectacular.'

'Then we have a surprise for you.' He kissed her lightly on the forehead. 'Wait and see.'

As he had predicted, she was surprised to discover that an entire stage moved slowly over the dance floor towards the many tables which were spread out on carpeted layers, stretching right back and to both sides of the huge club. Diners, and people who were merely sipping French champagne, were all rewarded with a magnificent view of the show.

Meredith had not known what to expect and found herself swept up as she watched the performance. Every step, every movement was planned and calculated, timed to the split second to give pleasure. The beplumed showgirls were stunningly beautiful, and at the end of the show, she gazed up delightedly as the beauties sat on swings, adorned with flowers, and swung outwards, over many of the tables. Amidst many floating balloons her eyes went to Marc and she found herself wondering what he had thought of her own bare breasts when she had angrily dropped the bath-towel that evening and, before that, on a very private beach in Mauritius. Was he comparing them now to those of the stunning showgirls? Their eyes met and held.

When it was all over she turned to him and said, 'I'm sorry, in a way, that I brought my umbrella, because now I will have to battle my way to hand in my ticket and collect it. There were so many wraps there. Did you notice?'

'We have all the time in the world,' he told her easily. 'You can stay in bed until quite late in the morning. I

personally will serve you breakfast there.' Their eyes
met and then Meredith dropped her lashes. His hand
was on the white cloth, long-fingered and tanned . . .

'Oh,' she murmured, 'I'll be up and about, don't
worry.' Her voice was offhand and nervous.

Marc came with her to the desk and, as it so
happened, the same girl attended to her again—and
remembered her. 'You were lucky,' she said. 'Your
letter has already gone. I got a stamp from the office.'

Feeling the colour drain from her face, Meredith
said, 'Oh, thank you, very much. That was very kind
of you.'

In the car Marc asked, 'What letter would that be?'

'Oh—a private letter,' she stammered, after a
moment.

'Very private, I should say. Why did you not ask me
about posting it? Thierry always keeps a selection of
stamps in her writing desk.'

'Well, what does it matter? It's posted now.'

'Yes, it is posted now. Who were you writing to?'
He made no effort to start the car.

Thinking about his remark to the effect that he had
not reached his present age without having seen the
naked body of a woman before, Meredith felt the
sudden urge to hurt him, as he had hurt her.

'It was to a man I know. You see, I also got around
before meeting you. I had—friends.'

His reaction was immediate. 'So? You had a lover,
in other words?'

'I didn't say this man had been my lover. For goodness' sake, what is this? I wasn't the first woman in
your life.'

The rain was coming down in earnest now and she
shivered slightly, for they had become slightly damp
while hurrying to the car in view of the fact that the
umbrella was a small one.

'What did you expect?' she asked. 'Did you think
I'm completely without—friends?' She turned to look

at him and, in the light of the city, his tanned face was all dark planes. His eyes dropped to her mouth, then he moved his shoulders impatiently and started the car. 'It is not important.' His voice was harsh.

Her thoughts were a network of anxiety and suddenly she wanted to tell him everything. 'Marc— —' she began, but he cut her short.

'I told you, it is not important. Forget it.'

'But it *is* im. . . .'

'I said, forget it! I cannot be bothered with all this beating about the bushes.' His eyes hardened, their dark brown intensifying to almost black as anger got the better of him.

Meredith was oppressed by a sensation of utter futility and turned away from him.

Thierry and Claude were in bed by the time they got back to the house, and when they were in the room Marc said, 'I am trying to understand what it is you want.' There was not a grain of tolerance in his face.

She stood looking at him helplessly. 'I don't understand,' she said.

'I think you do.' He removed his jacket and tossed it on to a chair, then began to unbutton his shirt, and when this was done, the shirt sailed across the room to join the jacket. Meredith's eyes were like great green jewels in her face as she watched him.

'Come here,' he said.

A kind of power seemed to draw them together, then Marc gathered her to him in a swift, almost famished kind of movement and they stood like this, swaying together slightly, before he placed his fingers beneath her chin and lifted her lips to his own. 'Let us start with this,' he said, very softly. 'I have wanted you—all this time, I have wanted you.'

His hands closed about her hips, drawing her closer, and she closed her eyes at the exquisite relief of feeling him there. He slipped one thin strap of her gown over her shoulder and then the other, her dress slipped down over her hips and he released her so that she could step out of it, before hungrily reaching for her again.

When he had undressed her he lifted her up and put her down on the bed, then got down beside her.

'Does this frighten you?' he asked softly.

'No, I—want it, Marc. This time . . . yes.'

'You are beautiful,' he murmured, and she caught her breath as he kissed her nipples. 'Why did you have to tell me about this other man? Why, Meredith? But no matter, I am more concerned with us. . . .'

A wave of hot longing swept over her, but she wanted nothing more than to clear matters between them.

'Marc,' she tried to wriggle free of him, 'I want you so very much, but I have something to say to you. Please, you must listen first.'

He drew back and gazed down at her. 'What is it? But never mind. Whatever it is, it is in the past, no?' When she made no reply, he said. 'Well, you have started something. You may as well finish.' He sounded impatient.

'That letter was to Richard Parker,' she told him in a small voice.

He seemed not to have registered. 'I do not want to know about this Richard Parker . . . come here.' He bent his face to her own, but she fought him off and sat up, looking down at him now, and a tawny-blonde tangle of hair fell across his face. 'Marc, you seem not to have understood. I'm talking about Colette's grandfather. I can't go on this way. I've written to him.'

Suddenly he sat up and his expression of naked contempt caused her to stop breathing and her teeth came down hard on her bottom lip.

'You have written to Richard Parker, you mean?'

'Yes, that's what I'm trying to tell you.'

'And you have given him this address?'

'Yes, Marc. I *had* to—can't you understand?'

'No, I do not understand and do not pretend to understand.' He stood up in one swift movement. 'That you could do this! As my wife, now, you could do this thing?'

'I want to explain. You must give me that chance.' Meredith looked round for her wrap—the lovely Chinese satin housecoat, patterned in wisteria and sprays of blossom. 'I *wanted* to explain,' she went on. 'Have you forgotten that a moment ago you wanted to make love to me? Have you forgotten that I'm your wife?'

'Yes, I have. One minute ago!'

When Marc was angry his words inevitably hurt her, and they wounded her now.

'Do not bother to explain,' he went on furiously. 'And as for making love, it wearies me beyond measure to think about it. There are better ways to amuse one-self than to make love to a deceitful woman, believe me. From now on, you will be safe with me—in this bed, and out.'

He gave her a direct look that appeared to sum her up once and for all, and dismiss her finally, in one brief second.

She watched him as he strode through to the bath-room and closed the door. By the time he was ready for bed, she had got into a nightdress and because she did not know what else to do, slipped between the cold sheets. When Marc got in beside her, he turned out the lamp on his side and rolled over on his side, not touching her.

'We will talk about this in the morning,' he said.

Meredith thought of arguing with him, but knew that, in this mood, there would be no point in it.

When she thought he was asleep, she got up and went to the bathroom, when she cried into her hands, then she washed her face, which was pale from weari-ness and strain, and went back to bed, careful not to touch him.

She took a long time to get to sleep and was awake again with the first breeze of dawn. Never had she felt so alone.

CHAPTER NINE

WHEN she awoke in the morning it was to discover that the sun was shining again. For a moment she could not remember where she was and imagined herself to be back in Marc's beach house in Mauritius. In her half-drowsy state, however, she soon became apprehensive, and something told her that although the sheets were surely made of silk and there was everything she needed here to be luxuriously content, she was troubled in a formless sort of way. Aware of the flower fragrances from a garden, she stirred, and then her green eyes seemed to jolt, as she turned slightly to find Marc, on his side, one hand supporting his chin, watching her.

'So,' he said, very softly, 'my beautiful, childish wife has awakened? You know, I have been studying you for the past ten minutes and I came to the conclusion that you are incredibly beautiful. It is a pity you are so deceitful. By now, we would have known sexual excitement and, what is more, great satisfaction. In a way, it is a pity I found out about that letter, no?' His hard eyes challenged her.

The space between them seemed charged with heat and she lay gazing at him. Sheer misery prevented her from answering him.

'What did you write in that letter?' he asked. 'Was it another bulletin on the wayside flower? What news did you have to pass on this time to the unaccountable sugar magnate and his wayward daughter?'

'Must we talk about that now?' Her green eyes were pleading, as she searched his face.

'What else would you like for us to do? Make love?' His torso was bare and his tanned skin was perfect foil for the golden-apricot sheets. Meredith's troubled eyes went to the mouth so near to her own.

After a moment she said, 'You said you didn't want to make love to me.'

He bunched his chin and smiled, very faintly. 'I said that there were better ways of amusing myself than making love to a deceitful woman. But you could tempt me.' He watched her moodily.

'Oh, but how can you say that? You're so strong-willed. You have such a strong character. I couldn't tempt *you* to do anything wrong, could I?' Her voice was heavy with sarcasm. 'I mean, you're of the haughty de Chavagneux family, and nothing could break a de Chavagneux . . . not even temptation, and certainly not a deceitful wife.'

Suddenly she sat up and bent over him, pushing him down. Her hair fell over his face and she brushed it away and stared down into his eyes. It was a strange and exciting moment and she experienced a quickening of her senses when she saw his dark eyes narrow and heard the tiny intake of his breath.

'It is ingrained in a woman, that a man must give in to her whims,' he said. 'But I have no intention of doing this.'

'No?' Meredith taunted him huskily.

He made no move to touch her, but she was aware that he was regarding her with quickening interest. As she bent to kiss him she saw his dark, thick lashes go down as he closed his eyes and he reminded her, suddenly, of a vulnerable small boy. Softly she rubbed her mouth against his and smiled faintly when she heard him swallow and she felt a great tenderness towards him. She knew that she was completely captivated by the trivial endearing things she had noticed about him and she would never stop loving him.

She kissed him, rubbing the tip of her tongue along his mouth, and his arms went round her. She tingled to her fingertips. There was a flaming of desire between them.

'Don't push me to the limit,' he muttered through clenched teeth before crushing her to him. Then he rolled her over so that she was on her back, and suddenly, the scene which had taken place the night before flashed through her mind.

When she slapped his face hard, breaking the spell, she heard him curse, then she sprang out of bed and stood looking down at him, her breath coming fast.

'You make me sick!' she exclaimed. 'This is what *you* did to *me*, last night! You—you didn't know just how much I wanted you. No, wanting is just for men, isn't it?' Her voice broke, but she went on. 'You—didn't even care! I wanted to explain about the letter first, but you didn't give me a chance!'

He grew pale with fury. 'Explain? What is there to explain?' She watched him fling back the sheets. 'You came to Mauritius to act as some kind of spy for this man. Did you care, when you agreed to pave the way for this man to kidnap my niece? No. But of course not. Of course you did not care.'

'And you married me to trap me and to punish me, because you're still living in the past—loving and wanting a—a dead girl.' Her voice broke again and she bit her lip. 'What use is a dead girl to you, Marc? Oh . . .' she shook her head from side to side and her tawny-blonde hair swung about her face, 'life was very sweet, very beautiful, very simple, before I changed my job as a laboratory assistant in a huge cosmetic factory and went to work for—for this sugar magnate, as you will insist on calling him. I learned the sugar trade and ended up in Mauritius. . . .'

'Go on,' he said.

'Yes, I *will* go on, because everything is true.'

'And of course, you were not without friends—without lovers? You mentioned that last night, I seem to recollect.' His dark eyes scanned the room and she was aware of his taut lean movements as he grabbed his clothes and threw them down on the huge bed. Her own eyes flickered for a moment as she watched him drop the short silk pyjama pants he was wearing to the floor and stood naked before her.

After the first shock, her appraisal of him was deliberate, insolent almost, as she intended it should be.

'No?' he went on, pulling on his trousers. 'Friends, lovers. A beautiful, very sweet, very simple life, you said. And now it is all changed, no? For the worse, hey? What made you change all this, I wonder? Tell me.'

'I don't have to give a reason to you,' she said, wanting to laugh hysterically.

'I have reached the stage where I should have reached my limit had I been a wife-beater,' he said.

'Really? Just you dare!' She spoke hotly. 'Just you *dare*!'

Sunlight gilded everything in the room, including the tanned sensuous lines of her body which were plainly seen through her flimsy nightdress, and the tiny tanga pants she was wearing beneath it.

At that particular moment a maid brought coffee and Meredith crossed the room for her Chinese satin housecoat.

Marc poured the coffee and began to drink his own, without passing her the cup which he had prepared for her. He was moodily preoccupied. After a moment, however, he said, 'This is getting us nowhere. I do not wish to be bombarded with any more nonsense. Reality is the order of the day. Let us face one or two things. You are my wife, but you are no better than a spy. In fact, you *are* a spy.'

'You have told me this, many times,' she said. 'I am becoming *bored* by it.'

'What exactly did you write to this man?' he asked.

'It must really savage your de Chavagneux pride to have to ask me again, mustn't it?' Her voice was like ice.

Marc was white to the lips. 'Tell me!'

'Don't shout at me!' she said furiously.

'I am not shouting, but then you are always inclined to lie, no? What did you reveal in your new bulletin to this man?'

He went on looking at her and, after a moment, she said, 'I wrote, suggesting that Richard Parker and his daughter Judy fly to Paris immediately, in an endeavour to sort things out. I told him that André was unhappy and that he wanted to marry Judy.'

'Who are you to decide what it is that André wants?' He was still speaking with scarcely controlled anger. 'As usual, you go to extremes.'

'I can't decide, of course, but I do happen to know that Judy wanted to marry André and that she's fretting for Colette. I didn't know that André wanted to marry Judy, but I've since found that out. Anyway, André had no right to take a tiny child from her mother. No matter how good a nurse is, she can't take the place of a mother.'

'Why didn't this girl stand up to her father? Has she no will of her own?' he demanded.

'She was under age. *You* know that. But I happen to know that Judy will soon be old enough to decide these things for herself, Marc.'

'I have not met this girl, but she sounds like a scatterbrained girl, if ever there was one. I will say this much for you—you at least know how to put up a fight.'

'*This*—coming from you! It's too much. I never cease to dream,' she said sarcastically.

'Okay.' He almost flung his cup back on to the tray. 'Okay, so we wait. *We wait*. Even if we have to extend our stay here in Paris. We will be here when this man and his daughter arrive.'

'And—André? I mean, are you going to tell him?'

'What do you think? No, of course not. We will go on in the same way here. In other words, you will continue being deceitfully in love with your husband in front of my haughty family—your words, not mine.'

'I'm sorry,' said Meredith, ashamed. 'I did not mean that. I like them all so much—only you drive me to say these things.' She shook her head. 'André knows you're not in love with me.'

'That is where you are wrong. André believes, very firmly, that I am in love with you and that you are completely forgiven for taking part in this affair. I told him that it was love at first sight. How I saw you standing there, with those crazy butterflies all over your very chic dress, an island cocktail in your hand. I told him how our eyes met and locked.' His voice was mocking. 'You must remember, surely? This was how it all began, no?'

'Oh, surely.' Meredith turned away so that he would not see the sparkle of tears. 'I remember it well—butterflies and all.' She felt suddenly alone and completely apart from the de Chavagneux family into which she had married. After a moment she asked, 'And so what do I understand to be the programme now?'

'What do you mean?' Marc snapped. He stopped on his way to the bathroom and looked at her.

'What I mean, Marc, is do I remain here in Paris with you—or what?'

'Have I not just told you? Of course you stay here in Paris with me. You are my wife, and you will return to Mauritius with me afterwards.'

'You keep telling me I'm your wife, but it certainly doesn't seem like it.'

'You are my wife, and it is a pity it does not sink in.'

They spent the morning sightseeing with Thierry and André, and Meredith tried to think of nothing else but enjoying Paris. Thierry took them to an antique shop which did not open to the street and had no display windows and was known only to important collectors. It was on the Rue du Seine, Marc explained.

At André's suggestion, they went to the Marais, on the Right Bank of the Seine, where he pointed out to Meredith the magnificent old houses which had been saved from demolition and which had been turned into apartments. This caused Meredith to brood on the girl Marc had been engaged to, then she told herself that she was gazing at all those places which until this moment she had seen only on television, the movies and photographs. Let tomorrow take care of itself, she thought, pulling herself together. *Now* was wonderful Paris. It was that bridge between Notre Dame, which they had crossed, and the Ile St Louis, in the middle of Paris. *Now* was being here, with the man she loved.

Over lunch, in the city, Marc said, 'I am afraid that you will have to amuse yourself this afternoon, Meredith, for we have a business appointment with the family lawyer. I told you about this, remember?'

'Oh, but Claude will be home early this afternoon,' Thierry cut in. 'He will show you round the garden, Meredith. It is really quite extensive.'

'That will be—lovely,' Meredith replied, feeling a little dismayed.

It must have shown, for Thierry said, 'Perhaps you would like to swim?'

'Yes, I would. Very much, actually. Perhaps I could put Colette into the water, at the shallow end? It's really very warm.' She glanced at André.

'But of course,' he replied. 'I am sure she will like that.'

'Colette is so good,' said Thierry. 'But you know, I

feel so sad for this small child.' She reached for André's hand. 'I'm sorry,' she said softly. 'I am going to love having this baby, but I keep asking myself if this is fair, André.'

'It is too late to ask that now.' André's voice was short and his dark, handsome face moody. 'She is here.'

Feeling her face flush, Meredith dropped her lashes. Somehow, the morning's sightseeing and the superb lunch seemed futile.

'I wish to buy my wife a gift,' Marc said suddenly. He glanced at his watch. 'We will meet you, in half an hour, at the car.'

Laughingly, Thierry said, 'What can you buy in half an hour?'

'I have already seen what it is I wish to buy,' he answered, turning to look at Meredith. 'Are you finished? Can we leave now?'

Her green eyes were faintly puzzled, but she said, 'Yes. This is a surprise.'

Later, when they were on their way, she said, 'Is this true? That you want to buy me a present, Marc, or is something wrong again?'

'Nothing is wrong. Come along.' He took her hand.

When he showed her the magnificent gold mandarin-collared, bell-shaped jacket which was embroidered with fragile pink flowers with gold centres and which had centre fastenings of gold brocade she gave a little gasp. 'But why? It's absolutely stunning!'

'I saw it in the window,' he told her. 'The pink flowers which appear to float, almost, reminded me immediately of that very elusive wayside flower. I knew you had to have it.' He was not smiling and she felt suddenly let down.

'I see. Was—that the only reason?'

'For having also to leave you this afternoon and to tempt you not to run away from me.' His smile was mocking, and she glanced back at the jacket in the window.

'I have no money to run away,' she replied seriously.

'But if you have money you would run away?' He sounded irritated.

'I didn't want to run away, Marc.' Her sunstreaked hair blew about her face and she brushed it back with one hand, while he went on looking at her.

'Good,' he said. 'Come inside and try this jacket on.'

'It's beautiful, but I don't know when I'll wear it.'

'You will wear it for me, over silk trousers, over velvet trousers—at sunset, in the evenings when it rains, maybe, on the island, when it grows suddenly cooler when we dine in Curepipe. You know, in Curepipe it is often drizzling and cold. One can enjoy a good log fire, even in Mauritius, where it can be so hot. Come, my darling.'

'You can be very nice sometimes,' she said, smiling sadly.

'Only sometimes?' His dark eyes went to her lips, before he took her hand again and led her into the shop.

In the afternoon, Claude Jourdan showed her round the beautiful garden and Colette, having awakened from a nap after her early lunch, held Meredith's hand, clutching a new doll which Thierry had given her with her other arm.

'So?' said Claude. 'You are going to swim?' They were approaching the exciting swimming-pool. 'I hope you will not mind if I do not join you. I have some work to do in my study.'

'Not at all,' Meredith replied shyly.

'I will arrange for the nurse to be with you while you swim, to watch this little one,' Claude told her. 'Oh, by the way, so you and Marc have decided to leave us for a few days?'

'Have we?' She laughed uncertainly. 'I didn't know about that. Are you sure?'

Claude looked faintly embarrassed. 'I can see that this was to be a surprise—I am sorry. Forgive me.'

'Please don't worry about it,' Meredith replied.

She was still in the pool when Marc returned with Thierry. He came straight to her and looking up at him she told him, 'I've had a gorgeous swim. So did little Colette. She's gone indoors now, with her nurse.' She swam to the shallow end and came up the steps, shaking the water from her hair. She felt invigorated and alive. Beads of water clung to her tan and she became a little goose-pimpled as a sudden breeze chilled the lovely garden, and she looked young and vulnerable. Shivering a little, she slicked her wet hair back from her face.

Marc stooped for a towel and draped it about her shoulders, his eyes never leaving her face. 'We are going away,' he told her. 'I have changed my mind. We will not wait for this Parker man. I have had enough and—enough is enough, no?' He smiled suddenly and his smile was absolutely devastating. Meredith felt incredibly elated.

'This comes as a—pleasant surprise,' she told him. 'But they might not come—Richard and Judy. Have you thought of that?'

'Yes, I have thought of that, and so I telephoned this man, and invited him to come to Paris.'

'Does André know?' Her green eyes widened.

'Yes.'

'I see.' Suddenly she felt flat and depressed. 'It seems I've started something, Marc.'

'You are beginning to shiver,' he said. 'Come, I have had enough of André's troubles. He must sort his life out now.'

As they made their way across the velvet lawn she asked in a small voice, 'Where are we going?'

'Do you know France?' he asked, with some amusement.

'No. This is my first visit—you know that.'

'So? Why ask? Wait and see. But in any case, cousins of ours own an ancient farmhouse, which has been restored. It is in the South of France. They are away at present, but when they knew that we were coming to France, they left word with Thierry and Claude that we would be welcome to stay there. It will be here that we come to grips with this marriage.'

'I see.'

'Do you?'

'Yes.' She did not look at him.

'This time there will be no slapping of faces,' Marc added.

'When are we leaving?'

'We are taking Thierry's car and we will leave first thing in the morning. It is near Grasse ... the fragrance capital, old, high in the hills, with narrow streets. You have heard of Grasse, surely?'

They were in their room now.

'Of course. I did go to school, you know, believe it or not.' Her voice was stiff. 'I'm educated, if nothing else.'

'You are also young and emotional,' he answered.

'I feel perturbed, though, at this latest development.'

'Why is this?' He sounded frankly annoyed.

'You *must* know why. I'm taking you away from your family, that's why.'

'You are not taking me. You have nothing to do with it. *I* am taking *you*.'

'I've been the cause of so much upheaval,' she said miserably. 'I had no idea ... absolutely no idea ... when I first agreed to go to Mauritius, the chain of events which would follow. It all seemed to make sense to me, once. But now it doesn't. Nothing makes sense. I feel so miserable.'

That night she would have nothing to do with Marc and cried herself to sleep in the huge bed, going through one tissue after another.

'You are going to look a mess in the morning,' he said in the darkness beside her, and making no attempt to comfort or reassure her.

'It's just too bad, isn't it?' she sniffed. 'I don't care how I look any more.'

'No? It is not so bad for *you*. You will not be looking at your face. *I* will be looking at it.' The tone of his voice was mocking. 'Look, why are you crying like this? People like you are always clamouring for some new experience—something new. And yet you put up a great resistance when you get it. Why don't you just settle down? Is it to get out of having me make love to you?'

He bent over her and lifted her into his arms, after first turning on the lamp on his side, then he dropped her suddenly. 'Ugh,' he mocked her, 'what a sight you are! I find I have no desire to make love to you, after all. You look very ugly, right now.' She knew he was smiling and hated him.

'You said your sister didn't know of my deceit.' Her voice was muffled. 'I take it that by now she does know? Claude too.' She began sobbing again.

'You are not married to my sister, nor are you married to Claude. You are married to me, so what difference does it make? Now get some sleep. You are becoming totally burdensome.'

In the morning Meredith's head ached violently and Marc brought her Codeine and poured the coffee, which the maid had delivered to their room.

Later, she studied the damage to her face in the bathroom.

'So?' He spoke from the door, leaning against the frame, with his arms crossed. 'It looks a mess, no?' He laughed lightly, taunting her, and she covered her face with her hands.

'Let me see what I can do about it.' He came to stand beside her and she watched him as he looked out a herbal skin tonic and creams.

'Why do you do these things to yourself?' he asked, filling the marble basin with cold water. 'What has become of the nerves of pleasure, I wonder? The capacity for play? What do you get out of introducing dismay into your private life? Come here, you silly little girl, and let me get to work on you. Tell me, have you mislaid the formula for leading an uncomplicated life? But of course, I realise that you feel threatened.'

'Threatened? Why should I feel—threatened?' She held her face still while he dabbed the skin tonic on to her skin, after she had splashed her face with cold water. She was only too thankful to have him help repair her ravaged face.

'The cause of most tension is threat.' He went on working with deft movements and her eyes travelled over his face, so close to her own. She could feel his warm breath. 'What you are experiencing,' he went on, 'is a psychological threat. That is, a threat to the ego. Well,' he lifted his shoulders, 'that is understandable, of course, for you have made a fool of yourself. It is for this reason that I am taking you away. While I have no sympathy for this Richard Parker and his foolish daughter, I have a certain amount of sympathy for you. Why should I stand by and watch this man see my wife humiliated? He had no right to ask you to do this thing—even if he *did* pay you well.'

'You have a terrible opinion of me,' she lifted her hands to her temples. 'Actually, contrary to what you think, money didn't come in to it. I wasn't paid a lump sum, if that's what you have in mind. I intend paying back my travelling expenses. At his insistence, my salary at his end—apart from what I was going to earn in Mauritius—was to be paid straight into my banking account. You simply refuse to believe me, but I wanted to *help*. Also,' she dropped her hands, 'the idea of working on the island appealed to me, I must confess.'

'Suddenly, I made up my mind that you should be

removed bodily from the scene of conflict. We have had enough conflict, you and I, no?'

'Yes.' She closed her eyes.

'Why did you cry like that? Surely you must have known what it would do to your face?' He sounded frankly amused, and although this hurt her she enjoyed the feel of him as he worked with sensitive fingers on her ruined face.

'Why do you bother with it?' She tried to move away from him. 'You're being cynical.'

'I do not mind being cynical if it will help you to see things straight and learn to control yourself,' Marc replied easily.

'It is *my* face, after all.'

'That is so, but I, on the other hand, have to look at this face, and I am a visually stimulated person. I need to be constantly refreshed.' He took her arm and pulled her round to face him again. 'Let me finish. Already there is an improvement.' He treated her with humour and nonchalance and she found this aggravating. 'And that is just as well,' he continued, 'for we must leave immediately after breakfast. We have many kilometres to cover.'

'I might tell you that it's a new experience for me to be constantly bullied,' she answered angrily.

'Sometimes you need to be bullied,' he told her.

Both André and Thierry went out of their way to assure her that they welcomed a showdown with Richard Parker and his daughter Judy.

'It did not take me long to see this, for myself, soon after you all arrived from Mauritius,' Thierry told her. 'You all looked so tense—so unhappy. André and this girl must come to a satisfactory arrangement, I feel. Did you not notice how much I talked on the way here from the airport?' She laughed lightly. 'I was especially upset by the look on your face, André. No, no, I think this is all for the best. So, Marc and Meredith, go away together and enjoy yourselves. When you return I am certain it will be to find that all is well at last.'

It was, Meredith found herself thinking, a relief to get away from Paris. She was wearing her simple, thin-strapped black silk dress and fuchsia-pink sandals and a matching hat to screen her face from Marc's dark, enquiring eyes. Huge sunglasses covered most of her pale face.

'You have made up your mind to relax, I hope?' he asked, when they were on their way.

'Yes. It's all I can do,' she answered.

'What do you mean—it is all you can do?' He sounded irritable.

'I mean, Marc, in the circumstances.'

'At this moment you are at your most infuriating, do you know that?' He turned to look at her. 'Do me a favour, please. You will now put everything out of your mind and concentrate only on this visit to the farm-house. I have not told you about this house. It is three hundred years old and very simple. It is furnished with antiques bought in Aix-en-Provence, Avignon and Nice. It is—pure Monet. There are peacocks wandering around. You like peacocks?' He turned to look at her again.

'I don't know any,' she said, in a small voice.

The breeze wafting into the car was delicately scented, somehow. On the journey Marc pointed out fields of jasmine, mellow red farmhouses rising from fields of flowers and roses and orange-blossom growing side by side.

They stopped on the way for lunch, then again towards the evening for a light meal. Marc had not rushed the journey, and yet Meredith discovered that she was tired beyond belief, possibly because she had been so distressed the night before. Her head was aching and she closed her eyes and tried not to think about anything. This seemed impossible, however, and her thoughts kept revolving around the havoc, which she had helped to create. She tried to think of other things . . . of Grasse, the fragrance capital, which had intrigued her with its narrow streets, and then Marc said, 'We are nearly there. You can take a bath. It might have to be a cold bath, until we become organised there. But it is warm enough. And then you can have an early night. You would like that, I think?'

'Yes. You see,' she added a little too hastily, 'I have an awful headache.'

'Why did you not mention this before?' He sounded more irritated than concerned. 'You should have taken some more Codeine.'

'They're—the pills—are in my luggage in the boot.'

'Why did you not ask for them, in that case? You know I would have got your case for you. No wonder I lose patience with you!'

'I'll take them when we arrive there,' she told him miserably. She had taken off her straw hat and her hair was blowing about her face.

Rosy-hued and rough-textured, the farmhouse seemed to rise, like so many other farmhouses they had passed on the way, from a flower field and, as Marc had expressed it, was pure Monet. Even she, who was so ignorant, she thought, could see that.

He drove right up to the huge front door, which was guarded by primitive ceramic lions, pockmarked by age. A peacock sat, unperturbed, on a wide window ledge.

'There should be a very elderly couple here,' Marc was saying. 'They live in a small cottage, but they will not bother us. They are helping hands. You can cook, I take it?' As he unlocked the door, he gave her an amused look.

'Yes. I would be shy to cook for a Frenchman, though. My cooking isn't good enough.'

'A Frenchman? I do not see a Frenchman about.'

'You know what I'm talking about. I mean you.'

'I am your husband. How you can madden me. What is this—a Frenchman?'

The feeling of rural simplicity continued inside and there were no decorating trends, and yet everything was inviting.

Meredith stood in the living-room while Marc went back to the car to collect their cases. A magnificent tapestry dominated one wall. Tapestry-covered Provençal chairs flanked a long, bleached table beneath the tapestry and there were two raffia armchairs, apart from inviting sofas and chairs. From where she was standing, she could see the hall, which had a white-washed simplicity and brightly-jacketed books on traditional Provençal plaster ledges. Pottery vases contained dried flowers. There was also a view of the dining-room, beamed and with a vast fireplace. There was another fireplace in the room in which she was standing.

'Well? What do you think?' Marc asked, dropping their two cases to the floor.

'It's very attractive.'

'Here, in this ancient farmhouse,' he said, looking around, 'I have always found that a special ambience can be created just by using lamps, playing soft music or by lighting candles. These rooms are not complete without lovers.'

Meredith's heart froze. 'Then *I* certainly don't belong here, Marc.' She was thinking of the girl—the girl who had died on the snow-clad slopes of the not so far distant Alps.

'I refuse to listen to your nonsense. Come along. We will, of course, use the guest-room.' He picked up the cases again and meekly she followed him.

'You seem very at home here,' she commented.

'Oh yes? Well, I have stayed here many times, after all.'

'Oh?' Her nerves tensed.

'What do you mean by that one small stiff word?'

'I mean—it doesn't seem to be you, does it?'

'In what way?' He was becoming angry again.

'It's so cut off from everywhere.'

'But no. There is much to do here, much to see. It is only a short distance from the sea and a one-hour drive from skiing. It is, in fact, very central to other places in Europe. You will see, in the morning, that we overlook Grasse and the Alps. I will take you to visit an enchanting village in the Alps . . . if we have the time and inclination.'

Meredith found her heart contracting at the words . . . one hour from skiing . . . overlooking the Alps. She had guessed, of course.

Marc had visited here, often, with that girl! Everything seemed to spin madly for a moment.

'This is our room,' he was saying. He put the cases down and came to stand beside her. 'You can see for yourself that my cousins have not marred this place with a lot of finery. It is a restful, sunwarmed place, and I want you to rest. You look so very tired. Tonight you will enjoy a bed to yourself—for as you can see, there are two.' He smiled faintly. Then suddenly he drew her towards him and kissed her and, frozen and unhappy, she closed her eyes. When he released her he said, 'I will make some coffee, but first we must get you something for your headache.' He resumed his authoritative tone with her.

'Okay,' she answered, barely able to lift her voice.

'In the morning we will swim,' he told her, 'and then we will eat breakfast on the terrace at the back of the house. There is a huge round stone table there, which completely encircles a weeping sophora tree. Many a dinner party has taken place—an evening's alfresco—beneath that tree.'

He showed her the bathroom which, although completely modern, was grotto-like and carved from the rocky terrain, he explained. Mirrored cabinets seemed to float above this rock formation.

'This is the only modern room in the house,' he told her, 'but even so, there are no modern touches, only basic textures and materials like cotton, linen and wool. Here there is everything you will need to pamper yourself . . . so, my little one, pamper yourself, while I go to prepare coffee. Or maybe you would prefer tea?'

'No, coffee will do very well, thank you.'

'Would you like to drink it in your bed?'

Meredith realised that he was worried about her, and this brought a lump to her throat.

'I'll—I'll come through,' she said.

'What, apart from your headache, is bothering you?' he asked.

She stared back at him through fatigued-blurred eyes, but did not answer. She couldn't.

'You do not like this place, perhaps?' he asked.

'It's not that. I'm just—terribly tired, Marc. It's all been too much for me and I'm feeling miserable, right now. Okay? I'll be all right in the morning.'

'Yes, you will. You will wake up in a mood as serene as a Japanese garden. Promise me this, Meredith.'

'I'll—I'll try.' Her head was beginning to swim.

They had coffee in the living-room and then she took a bath and discovered that there was indeed hot water, so she gave herself up to its scented warmth, listening to the music which came from the living-room, where Marc had put a record on the turntable. She wondered, wretchedly, whether he was thinking of that other girl . . . she did not even know her name.

When she got back to the bedroom Marc was placing a pottery vase on her bedside antique chest. The scent of pink and gold tea-roses filled the room.

'I went outside and gathered them myself,' he said. 'For you.'

'Oh, thank you! How lovely, Marc. Thank you, so very much.' She bit her lip and fought back the tears which threatened to come. She felt drained.

Nothing about her marriage to Marc de Chavagneux seemed real—nothing *was* real. Nothing made sense any more, not even the pink and gold tea-roses, nor the anemones, olive trees, fields of jasmine, roses and orange-blossom which they had passed on the way here . . . not to mention the peacock sitting on the window ledge outside.

CHAPTER TEN

IN the morning Meredith awoke first, and her green eyes went to that other bed where her husband slept. Marc was still asleep, one arm thrown across his eyes. Had he had a bad night? she wondered. As she gazed at him, an intense longing welled up within her.

Suddenly he took his arm from his eyes and turned over so that he was facing her, and for a moment neither of them spoke. In the flood of pure, shadowless light, Meredith's face was beautiful.

'You were very tired last night,' he said softly. 'No?'

'Yes, I was. My nerves were shrieking and on edge.' Her eyes were troubled as she looked at him.

'Why is this?'

'Well, because of the frustration of—oh, everything.' She was wearing heavy silk Chinese pyjamas in an apricot shade and unbuttoned at the throat. She sat up and saw his dark eyes go over her, and noted his moodiness.

As was his custom, he was not wearing a pyjama top, and she felt confused as she tried not to stare at the beauty of his bronzed skin and the dark silky hairs growing there.

'Marc,' she ventured to say in a tight little voice, 'you look so unhappy. Are you sorry you decided to come to this farmhouse with me?'

'No. Why should I be sorry? After all, am I not on my honeymoon still?' She realised that he was coldly angry. 'So,' he shrugged, 'why should I be sorry?'

'Perhaps you have your—reasons?' She felt an anger build up within her, that he should bring her here to this house, where each room must be filled with memories for him.

There was the sound of dishes rattling and there were mingled aromas of coffee and fresh bread, and she realised that in the kitchen breakfast was being prepared for them.

'I explained to you my reasons,' Marc replied. 'I am not going to explain again. We are to get to know one another here.' His dark, tawny-flecked eyes locked momentarily with hers. 'So? How can I be sorry that we are here? Tell me that.'

He flung back the sheets and stood up, then he went through to the bathroom, and when he came back into the room he was wearing white cotton drill slacks and a dark green sports shirt.

'Last night, before I came to bed, I went to the small house of the old couple I told you about to tell them about our presence here, and they insisted that she would cook breakfast for us. Tell me, are you feeling rested? Hungry?'

'Yes, thank you.' Meredith's voice was soft.

She saw the expression in his dark eyes change as he came over to her and sat down on the side of the bed. The next instant his arms were about her and he was holding her close to him. For a moment she resisted him, but then his mouth came down on hers and the resistance drained from her and then she shut her mind to everything else as she allowed him to kiss her while his hands moved in exploration of her body. Then he lay back on the bed and pulled her down so that she lay across his body, her tawny hair falling across his tanned face. She took her mouth away from his and gazed solemnly down at him. His dark lashes were down on his cheeks, and this was how she loved him ... reminding her that, deep down, he was as vulnerable as a small boy. She traced the outline of his lips with her fingers and, groaning a little, he pulled her down again, kissing her with an almost violent savagery.

'I want you so much,' he said. 'So very much, my

darling. I cannot wait much longer for you.'

After a moment she said, 'Marc, can't you hear? There's someone knocking on the door. Marc, quick! What's she saying, for goodness' sake?'

He swore softly before calling out something in French to the old lady on the other side of the door.

'Our breakfast is ready to be served,' he said. 'That is unfortunate.' He smiled faintly, but his breathing was coming a little fast.

Trying to calm her own rapid heartbeats, Meredith said, 'I'd better get dressed, in that case.'

She had intended to have a showdown with Marc, and yet just the opposite had happened, in fact. As usual, he had evoked a response she was unable to prevent the moment he had taken her into his arms and begun to kiss her.

They ate at the stone table beneath the weeping sophora tree. White lilies had been placed in a black vase and the place-mats were thick black linen. Attractive lounging chairs had been set about the long shadow-dappled terrace where white pillars trailed mauve wisteria. A low stone wall ran the length of the terrace.

'It's so peaceful here,' Meredith said, after she had been introduced to the elderly couple, who spoke only French, and breakfast had been set before them.

'I am glad you like it,' Marc answered. 'At one time, this farmhouse was falling apart. There was no water and certainly no telephone. It is, as you remark, peaceful, and an ideal place for us to come to an understanding of each other.' His eyes rested on her mouth and it was almost as if she could feel the pressure of those fascinating, almost chiselled lips on hers.

She turned her head so that she could gaze at the undulating countryside stretching before them.

'It's beautiful,' she murmured, 'and so near to the sea—which, because you can't actually see it, seems hard to believe.'

'We will drive to the sea,' he told her. 'We will take

food with us and sunbathe and swim all day. Would you like that?'

'Yes, it sounds heavenly,' she answered, before venturing to add, 'And of course, *the Alps* . . . the Alps are so near, you said.' She was aware that she had started to tremble. She felt used—and cheated—and pressed her lips together.

Marc was helping himself to a croissant and did not look up. 'That is so. They are very near.'

She swallowed, then said softly, 'Near enough to—to ski. You must have gone skiing from here, Marc. Did you?' She bit her lip and waited for his reply.

'You are a tiresome girl,' he snapped. 'I think you are baiting me, no?' His dark eyes were suddenly angry. 'Do not go on. I am beginning to get the picture for myself. So once again you are determined to put your own twist on matters, no?'

A wildness was rising up in her, but she had to fight it off . . . she knew that. The past was dead, after all, the girl gone. She, on the other hand, was Marc's wife; she had gone into this marriage of her own accord and she wanted him as much, if not more, than he wanted her. But what was more important was the fact that she also loved him—desperately.

'I was merely curious,' she said. The desire to reach out and touch him was almost overpowering. She longed to have him reassure her that, for him, the past was gone, but his eyes only showed frank irritability.

'Yes, I went skiing from here. Now are you satisfied?' After a moment he asked, 'Do you have something on your mind?'

Meredith nibbled at her own croissant, taking her time about replying.

'I—just wondered,' she said.

'I see. I am more concerned with—the present,' he told her. 'I suggest that you centre your thoughts on the present, if we are to get anywhere at all.'

After breakfast they walked about the garden and

Meredith admired the anemones and olive trees. The peacocks strutted around and a delicately scented breeze ruffled their plumes.

Later, Marc got the car and they drove to see fields of jasmine, roses and orange-blossom, and stopped at a small, rosy and rough-textured shop with those wide, wide sills, where Marc bought her perfume. They also bought food and wine, before driving back to the reddish-pink house.

As he lifted the parcels from the car he said, 'I think we will swim before lunch. You know, here we could quite safely swim naked.' He glanced up. 'With your tan and your hair blown about by the wind you would look like a healthy urchin . . . a very beautiful and exciting healthy urchin.' He smiled and his dark eyes caressed her.

Ruffled, she said shortly, 'I may swim naked at night, but certainly not during the day. Swimming in the nude is out.'

'So?' He shrugged carelessly and laughed. 'We shall see.'

While he was unloading the groceries in the kitchen and conversing in French to the elderly 'help', Meredith went to their room and got into a bikini, and was already in the pool by the time Marc joined her.

'The water is colder than one would expect,' she called up to him, 'but it's gorgeous . . . so invigorating!'

'Good. I have brought champagne,' he told her. 'I have also here a bowl of chilled Charentais melon which I think you will like.'

'What's the idea of champagne?' Her green eyes were almost closed as she tilted her face to the sun and looked at him. 'At this time of the day?' She laughed lightly, feeling suddenly carefree.

'This environment, I always feel, calls for champagne,' he said, and her mood changed.

She watched him with troubled green eyes as he set

the ice-bucket, containing the bottle of champagne, down on the table. Two crystal glasses glittered in the sunlight.

When he had finished he dived into the water and surfaced beside her, and when she started to say something, he placed his lips around her parted mouth and moved closely against her. She felt a mounting excitement as his fingers caressed her back and she tried not to think of that other girl in this pool with him, and the champagne which had awaited them. A girl who was like a shadow between her and the man she had married. Had he been with her, she found herself thinking as he kissed her now, when that girl had died in the isolation of those high, beautiful snow-clad peaks?

In the water, Marc drew her closer, moulding her against him. He pushed the tiny bra of her bikini up so that her small breasts sprang free . . . free and tanned to a rich golden-brown, then his lips sought their rose-bud tips.

She wriggled away from him and adjusted her bra. 'No, Marc, please! Not here—like this. . . . I think I'll get out now.'

'No. Come here.' His hands reached for her again and he drew her close and, for a long tense moment, they stood in the shallow end of the pool, their bodies so close that she could feel every muscle in his. His arms slid down to her hips, arching her towards him, and she felt weak with desire for him. For a moment she thought of confessing her love for him, in the hope that he might give her the news that she so longed to hear—that he had fallen in love with her.

'I'd like to get out now,' she said, 'and lie in the sun.' She pushed him away from her. 'I mean, this is really rather pointless, wouldn't you say, Marc?'

'What do you suggest, then? Shall we take the champagne to our room?' The desire he was feeling for her could be seen in his eyes.

'No, let's have it out here—just like you said. The environment, you said, always lends itself to drinking champagne at the poolside—and eating melon.' Meredith realised that the tone of her voice was hard.

She saw the expression in his eyes undergo a change. Later, as he poured the champagne, he seemed preoccupied and moody.

The liquid sparkled in the sun. Tensely she watched him as he lowered himself down beside her.

'Do you know something?' His voice was like steel.

'No—what?' She lifted her lashes and met the cold anger in his eyes.

'I am deeply distrustful of the future. Do you wish me to take you by force? Is this what you have in mind? This whole thing is filling me with boredom and irritation. You are out to tease and affront me, no? With me—so far as I am concerned, that is always a dangerous combination.' His hard eyes took her in from head to foot.

'Marc, how many times have you—affronted *me*?' She was so tense and unhappy she could hardly speak without swallowing. 'Or have you forgotten?'

'So?' He looked at her for a long time. 'So? This is your way of punishing me?'

'It's not only that,' she said miserably.

'No? Well, what else? You are regretting this marriage? Now that you have finally worked this out for yourself, you are wondering how you can get out of it. The idea of settling on an island with a wealthy sugar planter has lost its appeal. I have told you, and I am telling you again, that so far as I am concerned you will remain married to me. I have the power to arouse you and I have the power to keep you. Perhaps I should also put it this way—I have the power to arouse you and you have the power to arouse me—so,' he lifted his shoulders, 'what more could we ask? You mentioned a man in your life. Well, it is too late for that now.'

Before she could tell him that the man she had referred to was none other than Richard Parker, he reached out for her wrist. 'This sparring match with me is coming to an end. I have had enough.' His fingers hurt and when she looked down she could see the red marks on her wrist.

'Let go of me!' she protested, feeling an almost vindictive impulse to hurt him. 'You've had other women in your life, haven't you?'

'For sure. For sure.' He released his hold on her. 'And if you go on in this fashion, there will be others, make no mistake, but you will still remain married to me.'

Although she had practically gone down on her knees to plead for this hideous scene, the despair she was feeling was so great that she felt like breaking into a flood of tears. In a strangled voice she said, 'Please feel perfectly free. If that's what you want—go ahead. You act as—as if you've been virtually created for women!'

'No.' His voice was very soft. 'Not for *women*. For one woman.'

Meredith was chilled by the expression in his dark eyes.

'I see,' she said, her voice choked.

'No, you don't. You know nothing.'

'I know enough!' Her voice rose. There was a wealth of meaning in the words.

'For someone who has only known me a short time,' Marc commented, 'you certainly know your way around . . . or so you think. Do me a favour, please. Drop this.'

They ate their lunch at a table which had been set for them beside the sun-splintered pool. An antique teapot had been filled with wild field flowers.

Marc was tense and irritable and Meredith's nerves felt almost raw. She had slipped a caftan over her bikini and swept her damp hair back from her tanned face, and she looked dramatically beautiful. She had never felt more miserable in her whole life.

The scent of roses circling white columns permeated the air.

'Marc,' she said, 'I'm—terribly sorry about everything, believe me.'

His handsome face remained rigid, telling her nothing.

'I said forget it.' He reached for his glass and then glanced up at her. 'I do not wish for conversation.'

'Well, I do. There's something I must say.'

'Say it and then keep quiet.'

'I wish you hadn't brought me to the same house— *the very same house, Marc.*' She broke off and just sat there, shaking her head, staring at him . . . not trusting herself to say one more word, for she was near to breaking point. 'It's just—something I find I can't take,' she added finally.

'So? What are you talking about now? It seems to me that once you begin there is no stopping you.'

'It all fell into pattern, of course,' she said. 'So near to the sea, you said. *So near to the Alps. A one hour drive from skiing,* you said. This environment *always* calls for champagne. . . .'

'So? What has that got to do with us coming here?' He cut harshly across her sentence. 'I have not the remotest idea what you are talking about.'

'No? Don't lie to me! I wasn't born with limited intelligence, Marc. You told me she'd died in a skiing accident—the only woman—the *one* woman—you've ever loved. The girl you were going to marry. In other words, I—it did not take me long—to realise that you have been here with her. How could you be so—so shallow as to bring me here, to the same place—the same bed, the same pool . . . the same everything? It is amazing that you did not have some of her clothes stored here—for me to wear.'

He looked momentarily nonplussed and then he said,

'Meredith, you are fascinating, you are beautiful and you are exasperating. I have not been here before, with this—other girl—with another woman, in fact. I have been here, of course, but alone—a couple of times with Thierry and Claude. Once again you have shown yourself to be of imaginative spirit, no?' He settled back and studied her and his eyes were dark with feeling. 'I find this puzzling—your attitude, that is. Let us assume that I *had* been here with—this girl—you find this unsettling?'

'Yes, of course I find it unsettling!'

'So?' He was silent for a moment, before he went on. 'Why is this? It is interesting to—speculate.' His moody dark eyes never left her face.

'Why?' She shook her head. 'You have the nerve to ask me why? Answer this for me—simply by placing yourself in my position.'

'Well, since I am a demanding person, I should have strong thoughts about this. I might even give way to an attack of jealousy. However, I cannot see any reason as to why you should be jealous. Perhaps pride gets in the way?'

'Wouldn't *you* have any pride about it?' she asked, although she felt like screaming her jealousy to him.

'My pride would be in danger, certainly.'

'Would you be jealous?' she asked.

'Look, you cannot have it both ways. I have made it clear that I have not visited here with the girl in question—or, for that matter, with any other girl but my sister. Maybe I can now begin to get down to my lunch.' Marc reached for his glass. 'Forget about the past. Drink your champagne.'

Meredith made a pretence of lifting her glass to her lips, but left the champagne untasted and put the glass down again.

'You did not touch it,' he observed.

'I don't feel like drinking champagne. Now is not the time for champagne so far as I'm concerned, Marc.'

'Nevertheless, I opened it especially for you, and you will do me the courtesy of at least moistening your lips.'

'I'm tired of fighting you, Marc. I give up.'

'I am glad you realise you have lost.' His eyes were mocking. 'No, no, I feel that it is indeed a time for champagne. At last I feel that we are getting somewhere, you and I. Meredith, surely it is very unusual to have a beautiful and desirable body which has not yet been possessed by one's husband? And so I think we should drink a toast to your surrender—safe in the knowledge that no other girl has shared a bed with me in this house, or bathed with me in the bath—for we will bathe together, before we leave this house—or submitted to my caresses in the swimming-pool. Do you believe what I am saying?' His eyes met hers.

'Is it important whether I believe it or not?'

Marc became violently angry. 'What is this? You know it is important. You have gone to great lengths to *show* that it is important. So? Why ask? It is important to you and therefore it is important to me. The past is the past. The fact that I was engaged to a girl once does not prove one thing.'

'It proves you loved her.'

'I advise you to keep quiet about love. What do you know about love? Nothing. You send me into a blind rage when you mention the word.'

'Do I?' While she was speaking she was chiefly conscious of his eyes. They were as cold as stone.

'Look. . . .' he almost threw his glass on to the table. 'Do you wish me to tell you that I am madly in love with you, merely to restore your confidence in yourself? The confidence which stems from the belief that you are the one and only woman I have ever loved—ever wanted—ever touched? Or do you wish me to tell you that I am madly in love with you because this is what you wish?'

'Marc, you deceived me, when you married me.'

'In what way did I deceive you? You were ready to sail into marriage with me. You could have said no, but instead you said yes. You went into marriage with me with unscrupulous calculation.'

'You're so—uncaring,' she said, on a little gasp.

'No, it is you who is uncaring. You want everything your own way, on your own terms. There is no reasoning with you. I tell you, you will make the best of this marriage. It is up to you.'

'You married me merely to punish me.'

'If anyone has been punished, it is me.' He laughed shortly.

'It was a despicable thing to do!' she went on.

'Okay, okay, so it was a despicable thing to do. *But* I was aware of you, from the moment I saw you. I knew I wanted you and, what is more, I grew to learn that you wanted me. So far as I was concerned, that was sufficient. It can still be sufficient. I am no longer willing to curb my lovemaking.' He lifted his glass. 'Let us drink to our union. You will go through with it, whether you want to or not, do you understand? Or shall I spell it out for you?' He pushed back his chair, and some time later, Meredith heard the car start and realised that he was going out—without her.

She started to shiver, then tried to think of a plan—but all sense of planning was gone. She only knew that she could not live without him ... that she wanted him on any terms, but, woman-like, she had gone out of her way, again and again, to be difficult, even when she had been craving to be possessed by him, hurting him—and hurting herself.

CHAPTER ELEVEN

MEREDITH could not bear to go back into the house, so she slipped out of her caftan and lay down next to the pool. Although a strong wind had sprung up, the sun was warm and soothing and she felt she could smell the tang of the sea.

Even when the sun had lost its strength, she remained where she was, limp with the unhappiness she was feeling. From the outside, she saw herself coldly.

She had allowed Richard Parker to talk her into going to Mauritius to meddle in the affairs of others, and she hated him, now, for being the cause of her humiliation. She had floated into a marriage with a man who absolutely despised her and who at no time had told her that he was in love with her. Because of more meddling on her part, by the very fact that she had written to Richard Parker—when the de Chavagneux family were doing things their way—she was here, now, in the South of France, near Grasse.

Without opening her eyes she knew that the weather was changing, and changing rapidly. Then it began to rain, softly at first, becoming harder, until it was raining in earnest. Still she could not bring herself to get up and go into the house. She lay there, feeling exhausted and empty and very sad.

When she heard the car returning she bit her lip so hard that it hurt but continued to lie where she was, with one arm across her eyes. She could hear the sound of the rain on the pool and she had never felt such despair in her life. Turning over on to her stomach, she felt the tears running down her cheeks.

A certain time elapsed and she realised that Marc

must be looking for her in the house, then she became aware of him beside her.

'Meredith?' He got down beside her and turned her over on to her back, and she held her fingers tightly across her eyes. She did not resist, however, as he took her fingers in his own and moved her hand away from her face. Through half-closed eyes she could see the sky, which was heavy with rain.

'I have been driving aimlessly about the country-side,' he told her. 'I parked somewhere and I sat, just thinking. I wanted to be by myself. Do you understand?'

She nodded, saying nothing.

'But you are cold. Why didn't you go inside? You are shivering.' He brushed her hair back from her face with his fingers. 'I know something,' he told her, very softly. 'You are the most important thing in my life.'

Unable to control the tears that nearly blinded her, she asked, 'Why am I important to you? Is it because you want to—make love to me?'

'I can *make love* to any woman. I want to love you. I love you.'

'I don't believe it.' She bit her lip and shook her head. 'I just can't believe it, Marc.'

'It is true. I was in love with you from the start. You know that? That is why everything came as such a blow. I knew you did not love me, but I was willing to take the risk—to throw prudence to the winds by asking you to marry me. In a way I wanted to punish you, to break you down, that is true . . . but I loved you very much. There is a saying, no, that you always hurt the one you love?'

'Yes.' Meredith made the transition from misery to joy. 'There's a saying . . . there's also another saying. . . .'

'What is it?' He pressed his lips to her forehead, then drew back to look into her eyes.

'That a woman likes to change her mind. I kept changing my mind—about being made love to by you, but there were reasons. I felt—used up.' She began to cry again, softly, and Marc held her close in the rain.

'Do not talk now,' he said. 'Come.' He drew her up, then lifted her into his arms and carried her into the house and straight through to the bathroom.

He was soaked to the skin. 'I am going to run water in the bath for you. While you bath I will take a shower,' he said. 'So take your time.'

Meredith sat on the side of the bath, silent and sad, but strangely at peace, while the water cascaded into it.

'Get out of your bikini,' Marc was saying, and like a child she obeyed and stood naked before him. She saw his dark eyes flicker over her and the sudden swift change in them. He held her hand as she stepped into the water, which was frothy and fragrant. A window framed a view of the pastoral Provençal landscape, which was now blotted out by rain and the approaching night. Indirect lighting projected an aura around the mirrored cabinets that seemed to float above the bath in its strange bed of rock. To one side there was a shower stall with a glass sliding door, and she heard Marc slide back the door and, after a moment, the sound of splintering water behind the door, and she lay back in the scented water. There was an element of drama about the entire setting, but after a moment, she closed her eyes and relaxed completely. She did not move when she heard him leave the cubicle, and then, after a while, he came back. He was wearing white cotton drill slacks and a black silk shirt, open to the waist, and he was carrying two glittering glasses.

'I have brought you a drink,' he told her. She watched him as he sat down on the side of the bath.

Easing herself into a sitting position, she took the glass from him, her eyes on his face. 'Thank you. What is it, Marc?'

'Cognac. It will warm you.'

Her glance dropped to the glass she was holding, in

both hands. 'It smells divine. So rich, and what I need right now.' There was still a certain amount of strain in her voice.

'What happened to me with this girl—the girl who lost her life in a skiing accident—happened in,' he lifted his shoulders, 'I suppose you could call it my "salad days". I have changed since then, believe me.' He turned his head away from her and contemplated the rich, golden liquid in his glass. His free hand went to her hair and he trailed his fingers through it and she enjoyed the sensation. There was, she noticed, a touch of sadness on his face and his eyes caught little glints of the room lighting. 'You have got to believe this, once and for all,' he added. 'Otherwise it is no use. I do not expect this to click into place with you now, at this very moment, but you must think about it and come to believe it—for it is true.'

Her own face was pale from weariness. 'Finish your cognac,' he went on. 'There is a fire in the living-room. There are enormous logs burning there.' He laughed softly. 'Also, I have been told that there is a fine casserole in red wine in the oven, ready for us when we wish to eat.'

'That sounds—super,' Meredith answered.

He took the chunky glass from her and placed it on one of the cabinets and drew her up out of the water and helped her to step out of the bath. Then he draped a huge towel about her and, as his arms tightened about her, she began slowly to drown. Stooping, he gently bit her lower lip and, beneath the towel, her small breasts were stretched taut—and waiting. She opened her eyes and looked up at him with wondering eyes.

'Because of your involvement with this man Parker, I have gone out of my way to look for things in you to annoy me,' he told her. 'I took a perverse pleasure in trying to show you how little I cared, but it is only fair to tell you that I have been in love with you since the beginning. You passed a remark that I was of the

opinion that I was virtually created for women and, if
you remember, I replied—not for women. *For one
woman.* You were then, as you are now at this moment,
that woman. Why go on? Except to say that if the word
love has any meaning, it connotes, also, understanding
and respect. I have grown to respect you. You believed
that what you set out to do was the right thing—I realise that now.' He lifted his shoulders and smiled. 'Who
knows? Maybe it was.'

She began to cry then and he stroked her hair.
'Something you said to me, I have always remembered,' he went on. 'You said that your price was
high, like good art. Your price was love, not lust. My
darling, I love you. I wanted you at any price, whether
you loved me or not.'

'I did.' Her voice was muffled. 'I mean—I do. That
was the only reason I married you.' Her arms went up
and around his neck and the towel slipped from her
and dropped to the floor.

Her tawny hair was streaked almost silver in places
by the sun and her skin was deeply tanned and ac-
centuated the fringed green lakes which were her eyes.
The budlike tips of her small breasts were more than
ready for Marc's kisses.

The rain was coming down in earnest now and they
could hear it on the tiled roof. It was suddenly colder
and she found herself shivering again.

'I am selfish!' Marc exclaimed suddenly. 'All afternoon you have been like a half-drowned willow in the
rain, and now I keep you standing, naked, in the bathroom!' He stooped for the towel and placed it about
her shoulders.

She stood clutching the towel to her chin as he
turned back the bedclothes. 'Get warm first,' he told
her, 'and then we will sit in front of the fire and have
our dinner there.'

He took the towel from her and she slipped between
the sheets. The cognac had warmed and excited her

and, looking up at him, she felt the increasing agitation of desire. A silence engulfed them and she could feel herself swimming in it.

When he stripped and got in beside her, she felt an instinctive thrill of fear, but still she knew that she was at last free to love and give herself to the man she was in love with—and, most important, who loved her.

At first her green eyes widened as she felt surprised at the sheer physical impact of having him, naked, beside her, then she responded to the excitement which was flooding her. Marc's lips and caressing hands were taking command of her body and mind and she could think of nothing else but being made love to by him. She followed the dictates of his body and the responses of her own.

In the living-room, the flames in the fireplace twisted themselves into shapes of grace.

There was everything they needed to be luxuriously content in the glorious days to come.

After two days of cold, fine rain which blurred the outlines of the garden as in an Impressionist painting and which they spent relaxing at the fireside, the sun came out and they swam in the pool, or went for long drives, stopping to eat light savoury meals, accompanied by superb cheeses, red wine and fresh crusty bread. The satisfaction grew. Marc's tanned skin was a perfect foil for the white cotton drill pants he often wore, sometimes with a shirt the colour of the blue on a peacock's wings. He started to teach Meredith French and she seemed to walk with a new serene beauty and dignity so that people stared after them, wherever they were . . . two beautiful people.

They began to think about getting back to Paris.

'So,' Marc said one evening, after they had been swimming and were showering together before dinner. 'I think we go back to Paris tomorrow. What do you say? Are you ready for this?'

Her heart seemed to stand still for a moment. There was much to face up to ... Richard Parker and his daughter Judy, André and little Colette, not to mention, of course, Thierry and Claude, but Marc had given her a new dimension. 'Yes,' she answered softly.

'And then back to Mauritius, our small reef-ringed island of blue seas and lagoons, no?'

'Not to mention all those wonderful white and golden beaches,' she smiled.

'Tell me,' he gathered her wet, soapy body into his arms, 'are you happy with me?'

'What do you think?' she laughed. 'Don't I *look* happy?'

'You look wonderful.' He held her back from him and his dark eyes went slowly over her. 'Ah,' he said, 'I still have the power to make you blush—that is good.'

Marc was a fast, experienced driver, nevertheless, the glittering lights had come on by the time they reached Paris. From the car, Meredith got glimpses of lovely clothes in shop windows and people thronging the streets, and she allowed the colour and magic of the city to wash over her.

Everything was gorgeously lit, she thought, even the plane and chestnut trees. They looked so green, even by night.

Taking her hand, Marc said, 'You are so quiet.'

'Only because I'm pressing it all into my memory,' she replied. 'The fountains, the cafés, the shops, the umbrellas, even though it's night, on some of the pavements. To me, the Paris sky looks mauve at night, Marc, not black.'

'That is only because you are in love with a dashing Frenchman,' he told her.

'You're so conceited!' she laughed.

'We will be back,' he told her. 'You will see it all again. Before we leave for Mauritius, Thierry will take you shopping, and you must buy whatever you like.'

'Thank you. I feel excited at the mere thought.' She was becoming apprehensive, however. 'By this time, Marc, Thierry might well despise me. If things went wrong.'

'That is hardly likely.'

The lights of Thierry and Claude's residence were reflected in the pool and, once again, as she gazed at the stately mansion, Meredith was reminded of sweeping staircases with galleries, oil paintings and handsome bronzes.

She felt stiff with tension as she stepped from the car.

'I feel awful,' she whispered. 'So nervous.'

'There is no need to be nervous,' Marc told her, taking her hand.

Thierry, wearing a loose shell-pink cashmere sweater, and Claude were relaxing in the living-room with the pillow-laden sofas, beamed ceiling and white fireplace, which contrasted so well with the walls, the colour of the inside of a ripe watermelon. White flowers were banked everywhere.

Meredith's green eyes immediately registered that there was no sign of Richard and Judy Parker. André was absent into the bargain.

Thierry roused herself from the pillows, shaking back her hair and smiling widely. 'So? The lovers have returned? How well you both look, how *different*. Don't they look well and—beautiful, Claude?'

'Yes, indeed. How are you both?' Claude asked.

When they had settled themselves Thierry said, 'Well, this place has certainly been a place for lovers. First you two young things and then André and his little Judy. Would you believe it? Everything has been sorted out. They are going to be married. At first we did not like this Richard Parker—Judy's father—but Claude will tell you.'

'I must admit,' said Claude, 'that we considered him to be a devious and calculating person. But soon we began to realise that this man was very worried about his daughter and, what was more, his little granddaughter. On the other hand, he was not prepared for Judy to marry a de Chavagneux. . . .'

'Judy told us, in confidence, that her father is intolerable . . . no, what you say?' Thierry laughed and began again. 'She told us, secretly, that her father's intolerance and impatience are legendary on his sugar estate. But Claude, forgive me . . . go on.'

'His love for Judy is possessive,' Claude said. 'At first, I might tell you, he wanted everything his own way. But these two young people, André and Judy, are very much in love, believe me. He did not stand a chance, I can tell you.' Claude laughed at the memory. 'So the father gave his consent.'

Meredith sat stunned and disbelieving. 'And Colette? Did she remember her mother?'

'I think she did, yes. It is difficult to tell, really, for she is so young,' Thierry answered. 'Anyway, it was all very touching.'

'Where are they now?' Marc asked.

'They left this morning for South Africa. Being an impatient man, Richard wanted to get back. André and Judy will be married, very quietly. There is no doubt about it, he is a difficult man, but he thought all along that he was working in the interest of his daughter and her child. Everything has turned out for the best. A solution had to be reached. You must look at it from this angle, Meredith. You were instrumental—I think that is the word, no?—in bringing this solution about. What do you say?'

'I'd like to think that,' Meredith answered. 'I honestly would. Marc?' She turned to look at him.

'But of course.' He came over to her and kissed her lightly. 'Thierry, you must take Meredith shopping before we go back to Mauritius.'

'Ah, now you are talking!' Thierry's eyes slanted in Claude's direction. 'It will give me an excuse, also, to shop for myself.'

'It would seem that our Richard Parker is not the only devious and calculating person around,' Claude remarked lightly. 'But—in my own wife! Tut, tut!'

When they were finally in the guest-room with the huge fourposter with the blossom-strewn Scalamandré silk taffeta drapes Marc said, 'You know, my darling, you really do strike a responsive chord in me, and we never did make use of this bed.'

Meredith watched as he came towards her. Placing his arms about her, he drew her close, and her eyes closed as his lips sought her own. When he drew back to look at her she said, very demurely, 'What shall I wear? My fuchsia-pink satin pyjamas, with the lace?'

'No, no, that is not what I had in mind.'

She smiled her disturbing, provocative smile.

'What, then?'

'What I really had in mind was that short gold chain you sometimes wear around your neck.'

His dark, tawny-flecked eyes looked very directly into hers and there was a flaming of desire between them as he took her into his arms.

Harlequin® Plus

A WORD ABOUT THE AUTHOR

Wynne May was born in South Africa, ten miles from Johannesburg. At primary school her English compositions were always read aloud to the class by teachers, and it was generally accepted that she was going to be "an authoress one day."

Shortly after graduation from college Wynne took a position at the South African Broadcasting Corporation. While on holiday from the S.A.B.C. she met her future husband, Claude.

Tragically, their first two children died in infancy. Their third child, Gregory, suffered from asthma, and for his health the family moved from a place on the coast, near Durban, to the hills.

It was when Gregory was eight and Wynne was again pregnant that she decided to write. She completed a novel just before she went into the hospital, and after the birth of her fourth child she submitted her manuscript to a publisher in South Africa. It was accepted.

There followed an intensely productive period in her life, and Wynne feels that she had a kind of built-in strength that enabled her to cope with Gregory's asthma problems, attend to young Julian, run a home and write novels.

Wynne May's books have some of the most romantic titles in the Harlequin list—such as *Tamboti Moon* (#1343), *A Bowl of Stars* (#1691) and *A Scarf of Flame* (#2286). As for her stories' settings, readers may be interested in knowing that she once used fellow author Gwen Westwood's home in Durban as her hero's residence. Another of Wynne's secrets? Her age. "I'll tell anything," she laughs, "but never that!"

TAKE THESE 4 FREE
Harlequin Romances
as advertised on TV

Delight in **Mary Wibberley's** warm romance MAN OF POWER, the story of a girl whose life changes from drudgery to glamour overnight....Let THE WINDS OF WINTER by **Sandra Field** take you on a journey of love to Canada's beautiful Maritimes....Thrill to a cruise in the tropics—and a devastating love affair in the aftermath of a shipwreck— in **Rebecca Stratton's** THE LEO MAN....Travel to the wilds of Kenya in a quest for love with the determined heroine in **Karen van der Zee's** LOVE BEYOND REASON.

Harlequin Romances . . . 6 exciting novels published each month! Each month you will get to know interesting, appealing, true-to-life people . . . You'll be swept to distant lands you've dreamed of visiting . . . Intrigue, adventure, romance, and the destiny of many lives will thrill you through each Harlequin Romance novel.

Get all the latest books before they're sold out!

As a Harlequin subscriber you actually receive your personal copies of the latest Romances immediately after they come off the press, so you're sure of getting all 6 each month.

Cancel your subscription whenever you wish!

You don't have to buy any minimum number of books. Whenever you decide to stop your subscription just let us know and we'll cancel all further shipments.